D1421159

The Stornoway Way

The Stornoway Way

KEVIN MacNEIL

HAMISH HAMILTON
an imprint of
PENGUIN BOOKS

HAMISH HAMILTON

Published by the Penguin Group
Penguin Books Ltd, 80 Strand, London WC2R ORL, England
Penguin Group (USA) Inc., 375 Hudson Street, New York, New York 10014, USA
Penguin Group (Canada), 10 Alcorn Avenue, Toronto, Ontario, Canada M4V 3B2
(a division of Pearson Penguin Canada Inc.)
Penguin Ireland, 25 St Stephen's Green, Dublin 2, Ireland (a division of Penguin Books Ltd)
Penguin Group (Australia), 250 Camberwell Road,
Camberwell, Victoria 3124, Australia (a division of Pearson Australia Group Pty Ltd)
Penguin Books India Pvt Ltd, 11 Community Centre,
Panchsheel Park, New Delhi – 110 017, India
Penguin Group (NZ), cnr Airborne and Rosedale Roads, Albany, Auckland 1310, New Zealand
(a division of Pearson New Zealand Ltd)
Penguin Books (South Africa) (Pty) Ltd, 24 Sturdee Avenue,
Rosebank 2196, South Africa

Penguin Books Ltd, Registered Offices: 80 Strand, London WC2R ORL, England

www.penguin.com

First published 2005
2

Copyright © Kevin MacNeil, 2005

Extract from 'Late Fragment' from *All of Us* by Raymond Carver published by The Harvill
Press used by permission of The Random House Group Limited and © Tess Gallagher.
The Rika Lesser quotation is from *All We Need of Hell* (Denton University of North
Texas Press, 1995). Copyright 1995 by Rika Lesser. Reprinted by permission.
The James Thurber quotation is taken from an untitled essay published in
I Believe: Nineteen Personal Philosophies (Unwin Books, 1940, 1962).

Set in 12/15 pt Monotype Dante
Typeset by Rowland Phototypesetting Ltd, Bury St Edmunds, Suffolk
Printed in Great Britain by Clays Ltd, St Ives plc

A CIP catalogue record for this book is available from the British Library

ISBN 0-241-14320-9

*For tomorrow's
Lewis
and the Scotland
of next week*

*Someday we'll look back on all this,
laugh, then change the subject*

And did you get what
you wanted from this life, even so?

Raymond Carver, 'Late Fragment'

Author's Note

'For some people, holding a book at arm's length simply isn't enough. If you are easily offended, consign this book to the flames immediately, or return it to the shop from which you stole it.' So the man known herein as R. Stornoway instructed me to begin this book. I do so with an intense co-mingling of satisfaction, sadness, pride and regret.

R. Stornoway is, of course, a pseudonym. I made a solemn promise on more than one occasion to the *real* 'R. Stornoway' that I would under no circumstances disclose his true identity. His usual response to my promise was a drinksparkling stare and a smile that was fifty per cent sneer, fifty per cent entreaty: 'I know you're a man of words, Kevin . . . but are you a man of your word?'

I think so.

Anonymity in R. Stornoway's case is especially important because he comes from an island in which everyone pretty much knows, or knows of, everyone else. R.S. was thinking of his friends and family when he took the comparatively easy decision not to write under his own name. I think many people from a small island will understand – perhaps even respect – this decision.

The Stornoway Way is candid and provocative. Its loaded, intense yet pacey voice – ironic and tragic – recalls Dante's expression *vulgari eloquentia*. Furthermore, I think R.S. has written a necessary book, one that Stornoway (the place) has been in need of for some time, uncomfortable though that thought may be.

R.S.'s tone throughout the novel is unapologetic and opinionated. Critically (in all senses of that word), he describes a place that is much more recognizable to the average Stornowegian than the island paradise that tourist industry pamphlets glorify. So much the better, for local and tourist alike. For who's afraid of honesty? (A better question by far, *why* should anyone be afraid of honesty?)

Controversial as this book may be, it is none the less realistic. The Isle of Lewis generally *does* have a drink problem. Its culture *is* indeed conforming, both subtly and overtly, to the spread of globalization. It is a quietly vicious irony that R. S. – whose proud individuality and determination not to be culturally colonized are clear from the start – has written a book that is influenced at times by American culture and language. I wonder whether R.S. worked such designs into his book with a conscious and mischievous deliberation, in much the same way that he structured the book's flow around that of a bottle of whisky and its aftermath.

It took many meetings with R.S. to discover his purpose in choosing this particular pen name. Whenever I raised the subject he would laugh uproariously and refuse to share the joke.

One night we were sitting in a pub in our Hebridean metropolis of Stornoway scrutinizing an early draft of this manuscript, R.S. drinking heavily as usual, myself sipping at a soft drink, as became my custom. Suddenly he lowered his voice to a conspiratorial whisper. 'I've finally thought of a title.'

I was intrigued. Book titles, like book covers, are much more important to writers than they generally let on. (You don't give a child the first name that springs to mind.)

'Really?' I asked eagerly.

'Yeah, man. Check it out. *Sliding Down Banisters*.'

I immediately liked it, and told him so.

'Like it?' he said. 'It's *fucking genius*! What d' you reckon?'

'Well, it has an energy, an instant appeal – momentum – you think right away of a number of images, correspondences, you want to know more—'

'No! No, man,' he interrupted. 'It's *fucking genius*! Listen, a guy goes into a bookshop – no, say *you* go into a bookshop and you can't find my book. You go up to a sales assistant and what do you say?'

'I'd say, "Excuse me, have you got *Sliding Down Banisters* by R. Stornoway?" . . . Oh, I get it, *Sliding Down Banisters* by arse-torn-away. Very funny. Very droll.'

R.S. laughed over that for three double whiskies. It took me some time to convince him that either the title or the pseudonym had to change. ('All right,' he gruffly acknowledged, 'maybe it's just a tiny bit primary school.')

He kept R. Stornoway, and hit upon *The Stornoway Way*, which, as well as being an appropriate title, appealed to his confessedly hungry ego.

Some months afterwards, he would tell me what the 'R' stood for, and throw another perspective on things entirely – but that is for later.

The Stornoway Way is gritty, but it's pure. You'll enjoy it. If not, then, trust me, you'll have some kind of interesting reaction.

I came eventually to know R.S. like a brother. I carried him home more times than he could remember, I took careful interest when he wept with grief, rage, happiness, I held the hair back from his face when, after a three-day binge, he puked up – unceasing as a waterfall – alcohol, phlegm and blood, I lent (gave) him clothes, books and money, I cooked for him and, above all, I encouraged him, helped him fight his insecurities and tried – tried mightily – to convince him he was a truly decent human being.

R.S. and I talked a great deal about the kind of person he was – his own self-construct. In our chats he encountered a great deal of negativity within himself. I tried to challenge some of his self-assumptions by questioning the validity of certain elements of his upbringing (e.g., it's not his fault that Lewis places such a strong social emphasis on alcohol, neither could R.S. be blamed for the severity of his childhood).

In this book of significant episodes in his life, R. S.'s parents are noticeable by their absence. This is partly, I think, to protect them from hurt, and partly in tacit acknowledgement that the young R.S. was not given the direct involvement in the development of a self that is crucial to the healthy growth of any individual.

R.S.'s response at eighteen was classic: he ran away from his problems in the vain belief that he was leaving them behind. But in whichever country one lives, ruminating depressively on the negative aspects of one's background can only result in tensions between, say, constriction and freedom, depression and the need for elation, self-loathing and the want of love.

R.S. sought validation through his music and his writing. His writings in particular are imbued with pathos (of the inevitable, of the unattainable) and with a haunting self-dissatisfaction of the heart. He frequently described this book as being, 'difficult to write but easy to read'.

My first contact with the man who was to augment so eccentrically my perspective on life was through the intangible medium of email. I was living in Sweden at the time, spending a busy and enjoyable year as Writer in Residence at Uppsala University, Scandinavia's oldest university.

As all writers know, it's a fairly common practice for

emerging or 'wannabe' writers to seek counsel from writers they admire – or have simply heard of – regardless of whether or not they have met the writer in person. A curious practice – an apprentice plumber wouldn't ask a professional plumber for free lessons in plumbing techniques – but a worthwhile practice all the same, I believe, especially if friendships, works of art and other life-enhancing benefits can result.

Dear Kevin,

I'm the new you. Only more so. Right?

Damn fucking right an I'm right. Ha ha now I've got your attention. It's like this, cove.* I'm a fellow Leòdhasach,† about your age and well travelled – like the ol' man and the grandfather, twice round the world by the time I was 20. (Say hello to Loch Mälaren for me – fishing still good there?) I supported myself by busking – living off my guitar and my wits. All this time I was thinking about what Lewis meant to me, how it shaped me and how I could use that to benefit my art.

Anyhow, I've been writing through the years and I reckon I'm about there now. I've thought about it, and I've decided to allow you to see my work which, as I say, is the real fucking thing. I think good writing helps a person cope with adversity as well as bliss (which can usually take care of itself). This is the writing of adversity: cultural, personal.

---

* Cove: a Stornowegian word. Pal, mate, a male person.
† *Leòdhasach*: Gaelic. A native of Lewis.

Will I email it to you? Or post it? What's your address?
When are you coming back to Lewis/Scotland?
*Sin thu fhèin,**
'R. Stornoway' [He gave his real name, of course.]

R. Stornoway writes not for a muse (ethereal) but for the demons of compulsion (real, all too real).

Kevin MacNeil
2005

* *Sin thu fhèin*: Gaelic. Literally 'That's yourself.' A friendly acknowledgement of the respect one person has for another.

The Stornoway Way

by

R. STORNOWAY

Contents

3

Part Two:
EVERYTHING'S BAD FOR YOU AND
SLEEP GIVES YOU CANCER

Contents

Part Three:
A DEEP AND SECRET NEED

Prologue, with Whale

I awoke on my tenth birthday, after stormtossed dreams, to find that the deep infinity of the Minch* had spewed up onto the shore near my house the freshly deceased body of a whale. I ran to my friend Eilidh's house and told her to gather up as many saws and knives as she could and meet me down on the shore.

With a great deal of effort and a stolen chainsaw, our crack team of local teenage coves and blones,† thoroughly bloodied, finally hacked the whale's reeking stomach open. This was during the days of punk. Call it curiosity.

I have no regrets. That whale's stomach was a revelation. To be more precise, it contained:

two fluorescent orange life-jackets
a child's plastic bucket and – bound to it by seaweed – plastic
*   spade*

*The Minch: the stretch of water between Lewis and the Scottish mainland.
†Blone: Stornowegian. A female.

thirteen (empty) cans of lager, the old Tennents dolly-bird ones
oh yeah – goes without saying – an absolute metric shitload of
    gunk
a plastic detergent bottle in Japanese (?) script
a key-ring cradling a janitor-octopus's worth of keys
a leather toiletries bag containing a plastic toothbrush, a
    mangled tube of toothpaste and a silver razor
a small doll with curly blonde hair and no left leg
a large unopened tin of tuna fish

Eilidh cried; she felt sorry for the whale.

This is not the story of that whale, but in a way it is.

I felt sorry for the tuna.

F.FWD >>

PART ONE

*Come Again Soon When You
Can't Stay So Long*

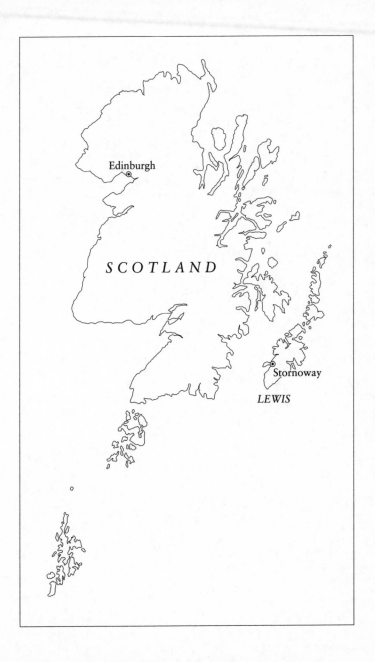

Learn Your Own Way to Hold the Map

Fuck everyone from Holden Caulfield to Bridget Jones, fuck all the American and English phoney fictions that claim to speak for us; they don't know the likes of us exist and they never did. We are who we are because we grew up the Stornoway way. We do not live in the back of beyond, we live in the very *heart* of beyond.

See I've learned the true meaning of distance now, at thirty, I've moved back home. (Still, I had to leave, to wear the itch out of my feet, or else I could never have come back, no?)

Here's the guidebook bit to get you occidentated. The Isle of Lewis once upon a whenever shrugged itself off the Scottish mainland, being that bit different, as all islands are or very soon become. A great and symbolic chip off Scotland's shoulder, the Island stands firm and unnoticed in the thrashing Atlantic. It's made of the world's oldest and strongest rock, Lewisian gneiss – ironically pronounced 'nice' – but Lewis thrives on its tougher foundations of guilt and anxiety.

Anxiety? It isn't just the salt air that makes us thirsty. I've seen how men respond to stress, I've seen how blood pressure's dodgy space shuttle or manic depression's nagging pendulum will smash the remotely sensitive mind into irretrievable black jigsaw pieces. The Western Islander's response to our diminishing way of life is that of the oppressed the world over, from Native American to Australasian aborigine: a powerful urge to drink oneself underground.

The sleepy sheepy tranquil hills and when O when will ye come back again glens of the Hebrides. Wish you were here? Fuckit, none of this is postcard pretty. Stornoway's the kind of place where the birds are woken by the sound of drunks singing.

One example of this gently venomous island's passive-aggressive nature is the way it seduces a person into routine. But –

Fact: for the heart to tick as monotonously as clock-work is not natural.

Fact: I swear, any complacency and this island will lullaby you into the grave.

Not me. Not now. I wake up each day when I wake up. I blast Faith No More's 'From Out of Nowhere' CD single on repeat, shower, dance epileptically around as I towel myself near-dry, put on my ragged punk tartan trousers and my yellow, white and fuck-you-blue *Union*

Jack Thalla's Cac* T-shirt and remember to live in
moments. I made a promise to myself (promises to others
don't work) three months ago when poverty – default
state of the Gael – forced me to move back home: I
promise I will as much as possible *feel* and not think from
now on. All right? Damn fucking right an it's all right.

I breakfast on sweet black coffee and outstare a book
I bought for its title, *All We Need of Hell*:

> . . . Twice resurrected,
> once detoxified, now delivered
> from a mushrooming fear of illness
> (my own as well as my mother's), I'd
> say it's clear: that part of myself worth
> celebrating came to life this year.

* *Union Jack Thalla's Cac*: Gaelic. A delightful phrase which doesn't
particularly endear oneself to England's royal family.
*Ah yes, Gaelic. The Language of Eden and infighting. There is a current and
inexplicably widespread misconception that Gaelic, because it is a language
of near-mythical age, does not have a vocabulary adequate to cope with the
most modern of ideas. For that reason, I shall be providing – free of charge –
among these footnotes, instances of Gaelic words that prove just how contem-
porary a language Gaelic is. Indeed, most of these words do not have an
English-language equivalent. I would urge, therefore, non-Gaelic speakers to
learn these words and to drop them into casual conversation at sophisticated
dinner parties, debates, business meetings and so on. Here's the first example:
aird-àsaig: the desire to do a job purely because, in your head, it has a cool
image. But secretly you know that if you did that job year in, year out, you
would weary, and ultimately find the effort, the routine, the realities to be as
unglamorous as your current job. Plus you would still have the same sorry
old personality. That's aird-àsaig.*

I put the book down and, as though it's triggered a button, at that very instant the phone rings. Seonaidh Shenanigans calling from London. Drunk. Stoned. Rambling on about how arrogant and rude the Londoners are. How much he misses the fishing – sea and loch – and how he'll punch his boss's fucking lights out one of these days, you mark his words – and how it's great I've moved back – he's envious, man – cos without people like me staying here there would be no Island at all – it would all be just English incomers (and they're a breed apart and long may they breed – *apart*) – all these English incomers patronizing us and destroying our culture and abusing our children and opening fucking traditional craft shops.

Good night, Seonaidh. Phone back when *I'm* drunk.

I've lived away from the Island myself, of course, and in more places than Seonaidh Shenanigans ever will. Travelling the world taught me not to hold the atlas the way it's printed. Everyone needs to learn their own way to hold a map. For me the Island looks better upside down, with our blood relatives in Scandinavia to the left, our blood relatives in Ireland to the right. Christ, even television programmes concentrate on English weather; they tilt the map of the D.Q. (= Disunited Queendom) backwards so our island – our *country* – is diminished. No bastard wonder we're the way we are. The most effective brutality is subtle; it has to be subtly evinced.

In any case, when you move away, you're still you for

as long as that's anything to write home about, but we'll get back to that.

I don't know what date it is, but I know it's Saturday. I can feel it. I hate Saturdays. Sunday – exfuckingcuse me, *The Sabbath* – looms before you, greyish-black, doleful. It's like falling into someone else's grave. Week after week after week.

I wonder once again whether I can survive this move back to the Island.

Eilidh lives five minutes' walk away. These days I no longer saunter along with a stoop, that spinal cringe, which non-Island friends attributed to these isles' habitual gale-force winds and which I now attribute to a failure of personality. I walk taller now, like a real person who really exists. Yeah, and I suppose it makes me look good; I don't mind admitting that. I just walk straight into Eilidh's funky wee cottage. On this island if you ring anyone's doorbell you're not really friends.

I haven't seen Eilidh for ages, and something quickens in me when her eyes brighten to see me. She gives me a hug that says more than it needs to, which irks me sweetandsourly. When we were kids we took all our clothes off together – the idea was we were going to swap over and see what it was like being the other for a morning – but we ended up drawing cartoon characters on each other with some purple lipstick she'd nicked from her mum. Then we started trying to make Minnie Mouse kiss Daffy Duck. Yeah, we've been through it all and have had an absolutely final *friends and no more I love you but like a sibling* talk. Twice, furchrissakes.

To be honest with you, I probably might be interested but for the fact of her bookshelf. It's lightly crammed with David Eddings, Sue Townsend, Terry Pratchett and others, the kind of writing that absorbs an eleven-year-old. Some people's bookshelves never grow up. I hate that.

She calls to me, flashing a semi-sultry look over her shoulder, 'There's a bottle of chicken in the kitchen. I'm going to grab a quick shower, okay?'

(Chicken is her pseudo-endearing name for Famous Grouse. If you don't know what Famous Grouse is, it's a kind of whisky – go and get some *now*. If you don't know what whisky is, then never, I mean fucking *never* try to bring me round to your way of thinking.)

Here's a question. Does a shower in any way constitute a flirtatious invitation? Unconsciously? Else why do people decide to take a shower when you've just arrived? This doesn't just happen in the films. Come to think of it, people have maybe learned the practice from films. In which case for sure there's a deliberate sexual invitation.

Be that as it is, I am who I am and there's no shower scene in this story.

Just as I'm about to get myself that drink a tiny movement catches my eye. Something comes skulking, grey, low-bellied, green-eyed – ah, skulking cutely, cutely – it's Fuzzy. He watches me steadily. I blink slowly and look away in deference, slightly hurt he doesn't remember me.

'Fuzzy!' I say, half-smiling, half-reprimanding.

Instantly Fuzzy pounces at my feet, gives a throaty mrreeeaaooow, then begins pouring himself in figures of eight around my legs, his tail swishing at my knees like a paintbrush.

'Ah, Fuzzy, course you remember me!' I lift his soft warm body up to my chest. His purring is the most soothing sound I've ever known; he purrs and purrs against my chest.

I carry him delicate as crystal over to Eilidh's couch, on which I've crashed so many times before, and I whumpff down into the soft cushions. I cradle Fuzzy in my lap. His purring is like a tiny engine. I wrote a song about him once, 'A Cat is a Geiger Counter for Happiness'.

'Course you remember me. I'm the guy who gives the best cat neck massages in Scotland.' It isn't for nothing that being a guitarist – i.e., being useful with your hands – is a sexy occupation. Hell, even cats know that.

I stroke and massage his head and neck, just as he likes it. 'Independent creatures, my arse,' I mutter, and mollycoddle him practically to smithereens, but gently. We enjoy each other's company so much it'd make you puke. I love it. But I also have to move him off my lap, sorry, just as he's dozing, because furfuckssakes a drink must be a-taken.

When Eilidh returns I've had a polite two fingers of whisky – dilution *in*cluded – but now it's probably going to get a little more dedicated, what with it being a litre bottle and all. Dilution of the first whisky is only to line the stomach. Water's for drowning in, not drinking.

Naturally, I'm not one to deny myself a sociable thirst.

Eilidh talks for a while about our schooldays. We're at that age – equidistant between school-leaving and being middle-aged – where we habitually glance at ring fingers, see mirrors as distortions and dwell with a lazy intensity on the perfect strangers we were as we thresholded adulthood. Eilidh enjoys reminiscing; these were her glory days. She was popular at school, bright-eyed, quirkily good-looking – in fact downright gorgeous when she was funny. Oh Christ, above all she was funny. Once, she saw our English teacher, Mr Snow, who was a religious man, standing on a ladder, painting the church on Bayhead, the drab squat church that's opposite the children's Sabbathstrangled swingpark. There was a stark sign outside the church:

REPENT AND YE SHALL BE SAVED

Eilidh, teenagely aware of her audience (me and two other guys) threw her head back and yelled, 'Sir, it says "repent", not "repaint".'

She was funny in those days. She also used to tell a great story about a dinner date she had with a chess geek, a guy she never saw again because, 'I asked him to pass the salt and it took him over thirty-five minutes.' Now her sparkle has faded, och fuck, if only enough for those of us who knew her then to see it for the fucking shame it is. Flowing black (twice dyed blue) hair now chopped into plain short swipes, neon-blue eyes turned watery and sad, snow-pure complexion now turning slushy with disappointments weathered and drinks assimilated. I harbour a grudge against God that Eilidh is turning into her mother. Eilidh – a supreme example of the *Leòdhasach** knack of wasting one's talents – works as a checkout girl in a small and therefore soon to be obsolete grocery store. She should be – but very much isn't – one of those girls who never has to wait in line, who need never learn how to change a tyre, who's always treated with admiration and lust, whose days are a charm bracelet, whose life is happy-go-lucky as a pink balloon in the deep blue sky.

Me, I'm a dreamer by profession (art, music), selling my autograph on a fortnightly basis to the dole office. They have no fucking idea what it's worth.

I like Eilidh best when she's being spontaneous, which she finds easy after a couple of glasses of chicken.

'Hey, Spaceman, let's go to the Castle Grounds.' She sometimes calls me Spaceman. I sometimes call her Pink Panther.

'Eilidh – it's after midnight. The Castle Grounds'll be

* *Leòdhasach*: Gaelic. As an adjective, pertaining to Lewis, God's own Island.

freezing and, I don't know, full of bats an rats an all kinds of vermin – pissed-up human vermin mostly – all scurrying around an stuff.'

'Shurrup, man! There's a great moon. We can take a walk up the golf course, bring the whisky, a moonlit liquid picnic.'

'I dunno. I'm not too keen. 'S nice and warm in here. C'mon, Pink Panther, we can just stay here and . . .'

Armslinked, fired up by a couple of large and fiercely convincing chickens, we stroll through the abandoned dampened streetlight-reflecting streets and eventually pass through the gothicky, horrorfilm archway of Porter's Lodge, which momentarily chills my spine. When we were kids some guy hanged himself there and all the older kids persuaded us – indelibly fucking persuaded us – that Porter's Lodge was haunted. This in itself, you know, has proved to be a kind of haunting.

Well. Maybe everyone has a place like it. Though the Castle itself is nothing but an image for a shortbread tin, built on drug money (Chinese opium), the Castle Grounds consists of one of those dark and folkloric woods that never really leaves you. Winding paths steer you round and round and up and down and – hopefully – back again. Trees all around you, unrelenting, every kind you can think of, thick, thin, leafy, slender, bossy, gentle, intimidating, reassuring. Then there's Sober Island – not really an island (you can walk out to it on a thin stretch of land) and not really sober either (this is where all the kids gather on the last day of school to toast their new lives). Many people choose to spend their Sunday afternoons wandering by the feisty, salmon-crammed River Creed; it's something of a Lewis tradition, since you aren't really allowed doing anything much on a Sunday.

The golf course by the Castle Grounds, though, swells with relief: memories are younger and happier here. Climbing its wide slopes we gibber and chatter about Christmas holidays we used to spend whizzing down the whitened hillsides on black binliners or ripped-off car bonnets, our makeshift sledges. (Nowadays, snow on the Island is rarer than a decent Christmas number-one single; nowadays kids perform Olympic-level snowboarding stunts sitting cushion-arsed in front of computers.)

We settle in a hollow at the top of the hillock, close and calm in the chill, and look up into the depths of the gloominous sky. The moon is all crisp and clear and chalky, like a tennis ball that's been dipped in powder – fuck, that's the whisky thinking.

Take it easy.

Eilidh lies back with a sigh. She gets tired superquick with drink, something I always interpret as a sign of general daily dysfunction.

I look up at the wide sky and remember when I spot it that Mars is visible these few nights. So there it shines and shines away, coy but proud, with a tiny, wondrous beauty, off to the side of the – of the *muselicious*, good one, file it away – the muselicious moon.

Pink Panther snoozes asthmatically, endearingly.

Aw.

Everything in its place.

As if God is made of gravity.

I turn to smile at Eilidh; she drowses, twitching sporadically, frowning.

The stars are far off and uninhibited; they shine with the tingle of a child's smile.

The bottle floats like the moon, three-quarters and waning, like everyothergoddamnedthing, as seen from here, God's designated place, the gravest place above ground or water, the place from which true beauty keeps her glittering distance.

Life Was Going to Be Fun

Once, when I was younger than I should have been, I made myself useful by taking Joe Idea, Karen Neònach, Jimmy 'the Tongue from Tong' and Eilidh – *seadh*,* Pink Panther Eilidh – for a spin down the Bràigh. This is how *a spin* took on a new definition in these parts, where even now it makes coves and blones of our era laugh snortfully and image up two couples windowsteaming that same old teenage car, yon patchwork Escort of Jimmy's that was mongrolled from seven other cars and was said to be the basturd graanson of a tractur an oll.

If I were ever to reach fifty – which I won't – this is

* *Seadh*: Gaelic. A multi-purpose word, usually means something like 'Yes, indeed' or 'That's right', but given the right intonation it can also mean 'Really?' or 'Yeah?' Sometimes little more than a space-filler (but not in this book).

Anrubha: *when friends start imitating – consciously or otherwise – characters from TV programmes, e.g., the ditzy one from the popular sitcom of the moment, the slightly camp middle-aged guy from the long-running soap opera so beloved of sincere housewives and semi-ironic students. Usually involves the repetitious braying of poorly mimicked catchphrases at decibels inappropriate to the context.*

how I would prefer to remember my longest-serving friends: young, decent and endlessly drunk.

Joe Idea – nowadays the pudgy, balding, divorced owner of a police record worse than 'Walking on the Moon' – was slim and fresh-smiled in those days. His long blond hair and tippexed teeth blinded girls to his beaky nose (like a crouched finger) and bad jokes (like, What did the O say to the 8? – I like your belt). Odd to think it now, but Joe Idea, in our day (in *his* day), was the girl magnet of the Western Isles. It takes real charisma to attract girls in the uniform he wore in those days: white hi-tech trainers (what the hell was high-tech about that pair of stinking gymshoes?), stonewashed spray-on jeans, leather jacket studded on the back with the Kiss logo, and, noosing his horizontally striped I'm-wearing-this-for-my-mum shirt, a Gene Simmons bootlace tie. Neat.

Karen Neònach – all mousy-brown hair and mousy, brown eyes – was an enigma and, to her credit, still is. The original party girl, she overcame her perm and Bon Jovi infatuation via her wild – and cagily sexy – laugh. Prior to the catastrophic death of her parents, more people had slept with Karen than had slept with a pillow. Many of them slept with her on account of that laugh, a tinkling waterfall of diamond-etched invitations cascading through the heart's letterbox. Nowadays she lives in a house she still thinks of as her parents', developing her knack for uncertain arrogance, dissatisfied wit and lasting inscrutability.

Jimmy the Tongue from Tong has taken his rebel-without-a-cause role too far by doing a Marlon Brando on us. At sixteen he was capital-H Handsome, with a plane-sharpened jaw and dark-watered eyes, cheekbones prominent as fists. During the intervening fourteen years he expands into an exaggeration of himself, enormous-shouldered, shame-bellied, always hunting out the smart black clothes that will make him appear slimmer than he is. During his disastrous years at Aberdeen University he took part in a crime scene reconstruction programme because he looked like (but wasn't) a rapist. There were crowds and crowds of locals watching. The Tongue convinced himself that the rapist was among them, scrutinizing him, and he couldn't sleep for weeks afterwards. He's a mean bastard with a soft and lovable selfishness.

Eilidh you know.

Me, I wanted in those days to be old-fashioned. I was less ugly inside. Not that much different on the outside – a little slimmer, maybe. I wanted to wear burly suits, to top them off with cool pinched hats at jaunty angles. I wanted to smoke moodily and constantly before lung cancer was invented. I wanted to live in an age of friendly manners and thoughtful gestures. I wanted people to be open and trustworthy, for thieves to be honourable, for shop assistants to be unfailingly eccentric. I wanted to exist within an early 1950s movie. I wanted to live in black and white.

Aye, well.

It begins by accident, sort of, as most good times and, come to think of it, nearly all bad times do. We'd been drinking in and around the plain stone shelters of our old primary school.

(Stornoway Primary. Those simple yellow buildings. Mostly my childhood was a wash of rain, but no fucker can deny the bliss of naïvety's warm and golden stupor. Somehow Stornoway Primary School was magical – that glorious place of yellow fun and blue sports days and forever friendships and endless football-high childhood summers and all that kind of unfuckable-with nostalgia that makes you blaze with joy and it's-all-gone-now anger at the same time. I was only sixteen when this Bràigh episode took place, but that very morning I had taken an unwitting amble up Jamieson Drive and through the sensations of my childhood past – the spicy green calm of aromatically mown lawns, the naked and plaintive fluting of wood pigeons, the pre-picnic scent of a car's hot leather and oil, the random thuds of a leather ball as it soared from one boy's wildly released call to another's: here's the impossible truth – in my early childhood it actually seemed as though life was going to be fun.)

*Co-dhiù,** I'm sixteen and everyone but me is drunk

---

* *Co-dhiù*: Gaelic. Anyway.

and the weather has taken a customary about face; the sky has scowled over and the wind has risen like a minister's wrath. We've a litre bottle of vodka, a drink I hate, and so, having lost my argument outside Cathy Dhall's for Southern Comfort (an aptly *sweet* teenage drink, no?), I'm sober. I couldn't take vodka in those days; it tasted two parts glue to one part petrol. *Seadh*, times changed, *tha fiosam.** My God, did times change.)

Anyhow, I'm shivering soberly in the November air, half listening to the others' excited blethers. Conversation is loud and predictable, though the teenage air fizzes with the electricity of invisible kisses.

– Man, everything's so fucking small.

– Did you see the chairs through that window – like doll's chairs?

– How the buggeration were we ever small enough to sit on them?

– Member how fucking *big* everything seemed then?

'Thrash on, guys, we're going to miss the dance.' I hate how being the sober one always makes you sound like the nagging parent. But fuckit, Einstein proved that time doesn't work the same way for drunks, so it's up to me to keep an eye on things. Tonight, it strikes me, what

---

* *Tha fiosam.* Gaelic. I know.

Ant-òb: *the sudden realization that clichés are true – e.g., still waters run deep, school days are the best days of your life – followed by the realization that clichés are also contradictory, e.g., many hands make light work, but too many cooks spoil the broth.*

we're doing isn't a pubcrawl but a schoolcrawl: carryout in the old Primary shelters, then a school dance in the Nicolson Institute, our secondary school. Education's a funny thing. It's like puberty itself, like leaving one school for another, forcibly abandoning safety and fun for anxiety and insecurity. At least booze is a cool teacher, opening the mind up to new ways of thinking and seeing.

Joe and The Tongue especially are absolutely steamboats by the time we reach the Niccy, and the 'bouncers' – furtive damp chemistry teachers on an ego trip – turn us all sneeringly away in their clean-spitting accents: 'Come back when you're sober. You're a disgrace to the school and your parents.'

'As if *anyone* can enjoy a school dance *sober*,' Eilidh growls back at them as we wander away into the whatnow. 'Arseholes,' she mutters. 'As if *they* were never young.' (They never were, not in the Stornoway way.)

'Next time,' mutters Joe, 'we'll just snaffle it in in some lemonade bottles like every other self-respecting underage alky. Or better yet, contact-lens solution bottles. That's the way to do it.'

We're sauntering along Springfield Road when Jimmy the Tongue stops dead in his meandering tracks (he's the kind of guy who can walk thirty yards down a five-yard street, once you've taken the sideways-nudging pink elephants into account). (He really should have been a tennis player.) 'Aw fuckit, man.' He lifts a glinting, dangling object from his pocket. 'I completely forgot. My brother gave me the car-key this afternoon. I'm meant to be driving home. Am I pisht?'

Eilidh sniggers. 'Does a one-legged Catholic bear shit in circles in the woods?'

Joe's like electrocuted. 'No, man, that's great,' he yells. 'Car's just what we need! We're going down the Bràigh!'

A shrieking of demented *Yeah!*s and *Aaaaarrrright!*s fills the night air.

'Well, you're driving,' says The Tongue to me. His eyes are all over the place, red and *gòrach*** and skeewhiff†* as a couple of balls on a ferry pool-table. He tosses over the key, which I miss catching by an Island mile, my eyesight being what it is in anything darker than daylight.

It's a reckless road, the Bràigh road, and God knows how many lives have been wrecked on it. There's an airport right next to it and somehow the Bràigh road itself feels like a runway (except, of course, when it takes a mad swerve you do not want to forget about else you can forget about *every*thing).

Despite the high winds and wonky, eyestraining, overhesitant driving, I get us to the Bràigh. *Any faster an you'll stop*, and all that kind of crap, but at least we're alive. The land is really narrow here, connecting the wet

---

* *Gòrach*: Gaelic. Stupid, foolish, glaikit.

† Skeewhiff: Skewed, all over the place.

Baileantrùiseil: *word for a useless, amusing fact that you resolve to remember – such as 'mother-in-law' is an anagram of 'woman hitler' – but will quickly forget.*

upturned hand of Lewis to the pleading thumb of Point, aimed like a rainsoaked hitcher's at the indifferent mainland.

Co-dhiù, the vodka's been meanwhile driving the others wild. By the time I've parked, they're all over each other in the back seat. It's crazy and embarrassing, and being sober and solo is super fucking awkward. I mean, Eilidh with Joe and Karen Neònach with The Tongue? Incestuous as a fucking soap opera. (By the by, for long years afterwards, Karen Neònach would wish that Jimmy the Tongue had been, this night she threw herself at him, 'a significantly smaller target'). The drunken backseat sounds like a badly dubbed porno movie, all slurpings and hoistings and gruntings and jostlings. I need the fuck out of here.

The wind almost rips the car door off. I have to strain bodily just to slam it weakly shut. Jesus Freezus. I close my eyes. The wind flaps and whacks me like a fat black towel that's been dipped in seaheavy salt. My face numbs. The wind unpeels my bobban *Hoi,** blone, does my tongue taste funny to you?* hat and runs away with it like an invisible *Marvel* superhero. No point in chasing it. It's halfway to the mainland in seconds. Fuckit, no point standing here shivering either.

Fighting the wind as I go back into the steamed-up

* Hoi: Stornowegian. Familiar (often overfamiliar) greeting one *Leòdhasach* extends to another. Like 'Hi', but with a sense of urgency.

car, I make a mild mental note to make a joke tomorrow about them being really – no, literally – steaming last night, and I nearly lose the door again.

The others barely acknowledge the Minchy* blast (up there past the Arctic and the Baltic on the blastometer). I rub my hands into something near warmth. I turn the car stereo on loud, then LOUDER. The Ramones. 'I Wanna Be Your Boyfriend'. Intense and poignant and absolutely the band that soundtracks lives like ours. Trust Joey Ramone to save your life; the music itself a kind of drunken seduction. I shut my eyes tight, then tighter, as the melody wispily reaches in under my defences. Just like Stephen King said about them, 'Some bands are tough enough to be tender'.

'I Wanna Be Your Boyfriend'! Was there ever a simpler, more affecting lyric? When the song finishes I hear the ferocious animal breathing of four hearts and wonder what we really *are* – hell no, *five* hearts – and where we're really going to, in this very *Leòdhasach* darkness, claustrophobic and fucktup and detached. Outside, the wind moans like the back seat. 'I Wanna Live' kicks in

* Minchy: pertaining to the Minch.
Barbhas: *the way time vanishes – you hear a song and can't believe it's ten years since it was released – and how its disappearance negates the latent comfort you harbour that you have many decades of your life still to live, thereby also negating the solace that, with the marching advance of modern technology, by the time you're old they'll have that artificial, eternal heart, that pill which neutralizes cancer, that sugarcoated eatdrinkdowhatyou-want superpill. Live a few more decades and you'll never die.*

and I reach over and turn the volume so loud the car vibrates in tandem with the almighty fucking whipping wind.

There Will Come in a Day What Won't in an Age

After the deep drowse of the boozed-up my brain's fog stirs frowningly. The ache, the tock, of the bone-white arms set at 11.00 a.m. on my bedside clock quietly alarms me, and there's a girl's voice somewhere in there, semi-distant. My head feels lighter than a junkie's wallet.

Clumsy-fingered I unpeel my eyes wider – a mistake. I'd neglected to close the curtains last night – or whenever – and the bright light of day is a white bruise on my eyes. By my left ear the young radio voice is singing with angelic pathos *'Mo chridhe trom, 's duilich leam'** and her voice is so mournful and beautiful at the same time it almost feels right to be in this near-hallucinatory condition – half hungover, half pisht – that we professional

---

Mo chridhe trom,'s duilich leam: from a beautiful Gaelic song and therefore typically difficult to translate. 'My heart is heavy and I am sorrowful.' Loses everything in translation.

Beàrnaraigh: *the art of passing off subtle lies (with sincerity) to tourists ('I swear, a herd of haggis went missing under mysterious circumstances right beside Loch Ness last year – now, I'm not saying there's anything in it, but . . .')*

coves and blones refer to as Saturday Morning. Being thirty, I've had about sixteen years of these Saturday Mornings. I unwittingly throat up a noise that is partly sob/mainly groan, and with a squashy pounding, all fingers and thumble, I shut the radio the fuck up.

I raise myself to a sitting-up-ish position, dizzier than a blonde on a hen night, and flop automatically back in the bed, the feathery pillow ringing my dissonant head like heavy metal. I wonder if yon weirdo from AC/DC's brain ever feels like this. Then again, strutting around on a stage in kids' schoolclothes nodding your head in a constant hammering twitch maybe takes a bit of brain damage in the first place. Fuck, my thoughts are havers. Today is off balance, a dream, that semi-unreal flow that brings with it a kind of running commentary in the head. R. D. Laing said that the uterine contractions of being born are like being munched in a mouth. That's how my brain feels right now. I need some Irn—

Weird. I sense someone else is in bed with me.

Fine. Great!

No. Not great.

I've no memory of last night. I edge a look at my bedmate. She – she – doesn't move. Long, glossy black hair spilled like paint over the pillow and upper blanket. She's snuggled all cosy and wombily into her (fucking

Beàrnaraigh-na-hearadh: *the sudden dawning of* – wait a minute, *have people done the same thing to* me *when* I *was visiting other countries?*

generous) share of the bed. I can't see anything of her face. I resist the urge to kiss the back of her head, though I'm already convinced I'm in love.

I have no earthly idea who she is.

I strain my pulsating brain, seeking clues of any kind from last night. I was drunk, a condition not unknown to me. Remembering what – if anything – Mystery Girl and I got up to is out of the equation; I can't even remember getting home. That leaves an ominous few hours of total eclipse. A fucking tragedy, when the fun that drunkenness is supposed to brew up evaporates as it happens.

What's the last thing I remember?

Nothing.

Okay. Been here before, many's-a-time. What's the first thing . . . ?

Going down The Star to meet Norm. Wait, no. Heading down there, I stopped off at Eilidh's cottage. Few chickens there, warm-ups, revving up to a neat, preliminary buzz. Walking steadily-ish to The Star via Joe Idea's new place on Keith Street, where we had a couple of glasses of wine, celebrating his new flat. Fine. We sauntered down Church Street, a bit giggly going past the police station, then stopped off at the Bank of Scotland for some cash – I've no doubt my wallet is empty today – Lord, just *thinking* about it is making me more fragile – then we went to The Crown for a swift pint or so before intending to meet Norm, the star of The Star, who'd have been raconteuring there merrily (more and more merrily) since two o'clock. But we bumped into Golden Shower and her lot in The Crown so we stayed there for a couple. And wasn't The Tongue there, buying Aftershocks all round, as he does when – and only when – he's blootered? Double Aftershocks. Dee Aye Oh, Dee Aye Oh. Down in one, you big screaming girl's blouse, you. So then – The Star, no?

No. God, my mouth is drier than a plasterer's pocket. Oh, fuck. Where were we? Aye, didn't we stagger up, arminarminaline – yeah – a bunch of us – who? – maybe ten of us – we headed up to OhmyGod The Thistle. Yeah, because the wind was getting wild and these wheelie bins – the extra big ones, the green industrial-sized ones – were being jostled and shoved by the wind all across the pedestrianized bit by MacIver and Dart's, and Eilidh just looked at all these wheelie bins travelling about as if by their own will, and then she just goes, 'Hey it's *Robot Wars!*' and we all – whoever we all were – just about pissed ourselves giggling at that, then Jeez, that stultifying pub. What about that barmaid – Bonnie – we've loved since she sold us booze when we were sixteen? (Be Buggered, we called her. 'Bonnie, phone call for you,' and Bonnie, slow and content as if barmaiding was a mix of comedy, therapy and beertap t'ai chi, 'Phone be buggered!' 'Cocktails? Fancy drinks be buggered.' 'Packet of crisps, issit? Crisps be buggered. 'S a pub, not a supermarket. Snacks be buggered.')

Be Buggered was great. Was she even there last night? Don't think so. And we couldn't have stayed long in The Thistle as we're really thirty years too young to be buying anything but carryouts in there, and the girls tend to be ogled there like way beyond even the filthiest of strip-shows *you've* seen.

That pool table, the one they should send to forensics as a curiosity, with all the unidentified spillages over it. Didn't me and The Tongue decide to have a game of pool before going off to The Star for Norm? I couldn't win a game of pool sober supposing my very fucking manbits depended on it, but with a few drinks in me, I'm the Pool King of Scotland, even on a wonky, sticky, beered-on, puked-on, everyfuckingthinged-on table with an off-to-the-bottom-left-pocket gravity of its own.

So I must have beaten The Tongue easy, I'm practically sure of it. Leaving The Thistle is a blur – hell, not even a blur, it's just non-existent. But leave we must have, because the next thing I know we're in The Heb fur-fuckssakes and I know I'm drunk cos I'm actually *dancing*. And not just the usual *Leòdhasach* IndieKid Shuffle, this is the full-on drunk epileptic punk on an invisible trampoline. I'm usually so pissed, convincing my limbs to dance is like trying to round up mice at a crossroads. Man, no word of a lie, people on fire move better than me. But I was on the dancefloor for what must have been ages, giving it stacks, even doing the hand motions to that Rage Against the Machine song, the one that goes 'Fuck you, dum dum di dum dum something something, something'; the accompanying hand gestures are like a fucking manual version of Tourette's syndrome and many's a bloody fight they've started inside and therefore outside The Heb. Last night, though? Usual: guys giving coyote smiles everywhere, guys clubbing girls with shallow interrogations. Trouble? I think I'd been in good form earlier, witty and with that nerve-free perfect timing, the consummate drink-encouraged comedian.

There was no trouble.

Really?

Uh . . .

It was a Dali world of swirling lights and eager maidenly faces like out of the old Gaelic songs, girls apple-cheeked and pale as the moon, yeah, even under that gyrating kaleidoscope like a bombed rainbow of lights and the boomboomboom of shoeshaking fatass rock-heavy bass. I think – yes, oh yes! – I even danced to the Sex Pistols' 'Anarchy in the UK' – it was one big blissful maelstrom. Didn't I even request it? For a girl? A blonde young thing in one of those *All of this and brains too* T-shirts. I remember her drinkblurred smiles. That dance *must* have been pretty fucking heavenly.

As Homer said (the yellow three-fingered one, not the *Odyssey* one, who never existed): 'Beer. The cause of – and solution to – all of life's problems.'

All else being equal, the blonde vanished into space never to be seen again. I got over the loss with a little counselling from Messrs Whyte & Mackay, and two minutes later I was jackinaboxing with the lads to Astrid's* 'Just One Name' after The Tongue threatened to 'hang the fucking DJ' to his face if he didn't play 'something that says something to me about my life'. Followed by 'Distance', one of the best songs ever written. Then – must have been near the end – it was the Pistols again with 'Pretty Vacant', the whole crowd of us blasting out that chorus, that gorgeous, venomously plosive final syllable, girls loudest of all. Everyone was so drunk and everywhere was pure volume and everything was pure out-of-it-ness, And then –

Nothing. Void.

Utter zilchness.

We surely never headed next door to The Star cos once you're in The Heb you're too much in the company of nicotinagers, underage overdrinkers, fashion babes who're barely dressed – you'll never make it out until throwing-out or throwing-up time.

But this girl who's lying beside me – she's having a truly monumental sleep. Usually a girl in a sleep like this, so deep it makes the Minch seem puddle-shallow, will snore – you know, all kittenlike and cute – and that sets a sugarbuzz fizzing through my heart. But this girl is just dead to the world. Pray to God, bow towards Mecca, light incense to the Buddha, chant for Ganesh, sarin-attack a

---

* Astrid, RIP.

43

few subways for the Aum fuckers and hope to Christ she wasn't trying to match me drink for drink. Cos in that case she *is* dead.

Och, fuckit, bless her. I hope she's having stupendous dreams, maybe of diamond ballgowns and glittering clifftop castles and golden tigresses thundering along naked beaches, and maybe she's swimming whitely through the sky on a winged horse, surveying her pastel-tranquil world and there are pink roses like innocent kisses in her silken hair and the air all around her wherever she goes is exactly the temperature of a wraparound hug. Bless her.

I'm in love.

She's a couple of inches smaller than me. No one I know on the Island has hair this fine. I can't resist, take a soft rub of it in my fingers. Her hair's so smooth I half expect my coldsweating fingers to stain it permanently.

I slowly raise the blanket and gaze at her – pure and unblemished – back and side; her warmth emanates almost visibly and the roomchill that funnels in under the uplifted blanket immediately forces me to cosy it back around her. I inhale her sleeping, its warm spiciness. I'd give my whole CD collection just to be this blanket for five minutes. Jeez, what did she and I *do* last night?

Bràgair: *word for when, on meeting someone, you instantly decide whether or not your potential relationship deserves effort, e.g., do you want to be this person's most fabulously witty friend, or is your relationship going to be too short to bother much?*

Truly, Mr Jesus H. Christ, thou art a vengeful God. Let me remember what she and I did last night and I swear on my future in-laws' grave I'll give up this dissolute troubadour life and go join a nunnery . . .

Nope.

Blankety fucking blank.

All expectations are false, I've long known that. But for something so immediate to lose not only its clarity but its essence – that's evidence of a fucked-up world, a world that's not just furious but sorrowful, too. Right? Damn fucking right an I'm right. And that's just wrong.

With a sigh I close my eyes and try to motivate my body to tell me something. A stretch of the legs is grey and weary. A deep breath punches up a delicate balloon in my chest; my breath is narrow and wheezy, crispy leaves scuttering through a claustrophobic dead-end street. My pectoral muscles ache, as always, like twin fucking heart attacks. My brain – as it does most mornings – weeps with thirst.

I attempt semi-seriously an experiment in auto-suggestion or hypnotism or whatever the fuck. I whisper in her ear, the magical seven times, 'The next time you see me you will say, "Hey, I wanna be your girlfriend, you default to perfect."' I whisper it gently and like magic her skin goosebumps. A good omen.

I smile and clamber delicately out of bed, determined not to waken the Dark Princess. My toes brush a soft something and I crab it with my foot up towards me, guessing rightly that it's yesterday's *drais*.* Naturally, they'll have to do. I slip them on, actively concentrating on my balance. I find and put on my glasses, since my hand-eye co-ordination isn't quite up to contact lenses yet. The glasses help, but not as much as a couple of whisky-filled ones would. Still, as the room's flotsam and jetsam settles into something near clarity, I notice with surprised approval her expensive black panties and bra, silk-shiny like her hair. Visual viagra.

Faded jeans and an old green checked shirt are enough for my inexplicably scratched arms and legs. Pulling boots on – that odd sense of rebelliousness, that pure coolness, is always nice on sockless feet – I determine to make it down to the nearby Co-Op. I'll do my best. Ha – maybe that's why in Lewis we call it the Cope. Not funny. On with it. Right, top of the menu Irn Bru (in Gaelic *Irn Bruchd*),† but if this girl is anything like I hope, then I'll treat her to a huge nutritious breakfast and I'll listen to her every word like a priest with deep Johnny Depp eyes, then respond to her like the Dalai Lama, with occasional reflections of Oscar Wilde wit while of course underlining it with the Sean Connery mix of gravitas and twinklyeyed mischief.

A long breakfast, the more time to get to know her (and, therefore, to learn about last night's shenanigans).

* *Drais*: Gaelic. Pants, unless you're American. Underwear.
† *Bruchd*: Gaelic. A little wordplay there for the Gaelic speaker. Otherwise it just ain't funny.

If she's a really classy girl – what the fuck's she doing here? Was my wit *so* much in form last night? Doubtful – but definitely within the realms of possibility.

And if she isn't *perfectly* classy – well, life is hurtful enough for all of us.

I plank a fishing hat on my head to hide the hairdon't, then sneak down the stairs like the invisible man has learned Shaolin monk stealth techniques. I close the front door behind me quietly like it just gave a gentle lick around its lips in the middle of a pleasant dream.

The fresh Stornoway air is invigorating as a cool shower. I feel guilty about shopping at a big supermarket, but I can't face Eilidh, who's working today. I perk up slightly on the way to the Cope, the more so as I plan Her privileged breakfast. So. Irn Bru, definitely: as Scotland's Other National Drink it relieves the ailments bestowed upon one by Scotland's First National Drink. Eggs – for my famous scrambled eggs recipe. Bread for toasting and/or some cinnamon bagels. Both, dammit! Orange juice – the expensive, bitty kind. Some Ibuprofen in case she's not a regular drinker. Some porridge – and that means I'll need milk. Plus yoghurt. I've got three kinds of coffee in already, of course – essential for teasing the

Càrlabhagh: *day-to-day ways in which a person is penalized because of public perceptions of their job. The headmaster whose car tyres are deliberately deflated. Or the cops in NYC who are often off sick because of food poisoning (caterers spit in their burgers and coffee, lick their doughnuts, piss in their soup, etc.).*

47

brain out of its muggy sleeping bag each day. Plus sugar.
Tea? I have green tea. Find normal tea.

Despite the parentally harsh lights and the dismal
domesticity of a Saturday morning in the Cope, I get
the breakfast treats within only five or six moderately
dizzying circuits. The queue is long, but not so bad by
supermarket standards. Slouching into line, I drift into
a hangover-encouraged daydream-film of that Tobias
Wolff story, I think it's called 'Bullet in the Brain'. The
one where the guy – I think he's a critic – gets shot
through the head for making smartarse remarks to some
bankrobbers. Then somehow it flips over into thinking
about how embarrassing it would be to die of a hangover
in a supermarket queue. I gaze into my basket – unnatu-
rally heavy in my drink- and/or girl-weakened arms –
and every product screams *Pishtup Cove Done Good, Beat
the Odds, Scored Undeserved Success with Far Out of His
League Super-Blone*.

Seems the witch at the till has been screeching NEXT
at me so I revive and soon-ish I'm whistling jauntily as
I pack the couple of plastic bags and leave the Cope's
warmth for the brisk walk home.

When I reach the house I decide not to wake her up,
but instead to let the homely aroma of coffee and toast
and eggs bring her round, then this episode will climax
when I bring her a gorgeously loaded breakfast tray. I've
nicked a rose from next door's garden, and this yellow
bloom is the final perfection. Its scent is heavy and clean

and dewy, and seems to revive in my brain memories of sunlit days, boys chasing girls in an air that shimmered with heat-haze and shrieks of stolen laughter. Boys chasing girls, girls chasing boys. Wild giggling. Illicit kisses. I love the natural neon of flowers. The rose, intense as a scrunched-up sun, physically exudes joy, in its girlish smell and blissful colour. The rose's yellow is a very yellow yellow. A yellow yellower than the yellowest essence of yellowness. The yellowest of yellows, a yellow so yellow it's way beyond yellow. A yummy summery yes-ness of yellow.

Aaaah, yesss!

Twenty minutes later, grinning with excitement, I climb the stairs with a joyous shake in my arms.

The bedroom has a lovely scent of flowery sweat and she

is gone.

I ate up the whole breakfast myself, then spent two hours in the bog puking up streams of chunky bile, feeling sorry for myself and for the curious mendacity of humankind. Aye, we set forth in joy and in sadness we return. The unremembered pleasures of the night no more than another diminution of the self.

All that came back to me was her accent, but not the words themselves, and it has resided in my head since like a wasp in a jar.

Sometimes I catch a whiff of perfume – maybe it's just a chance mingling of coffee and Saturday morning life – but I feel a little tug of yearning inside, a kind of warmth. But, as my friend Moses once said, a little warmth is precious; it will emphasize a scent.

And as I reminded him, it will also therefore disperse it. Life is hurtful enough. More than.

A Gossip's Mouth Is the Devil's Postbag

What happens on this island lies in stagnant tension between nothing and something so irritating you wish it *were* nothing. More so if you have a hunger – a starvation – to love someone with everything physical and emotional you've got.

Even legitimate scientists have proved that the brain often confuses hunger and thirst. But, am I right? – they forgot to prove that thirst itself is often confused with a thirst for *something* or *someone*. Damn fucking right an I'm right.

So you'll understand I get lonely sometimes. Depressed. If you live on a bleak weatherfucked rock in the Atlantic your days are mostly grey – and I mean that literally. My rain-flogged storms that knock trees down like matchsticks are actual rainstorms before they are metaphorical fucking rainstorms. Rainfall, rainfall to break the toughest spirit. A guy has to face it – life in Lewis is composed of days that are mostly B sides.

On this island it's impossible and probably illegal to

reinvent yourself, which is precisely why that is what I have done.

When I'm alone at home I have too much time and I fall into the old trap of thinking. It'll get you every time. I pour myself a drink – either Trawler Rum or a wallet-related quality of whisky – it doesn't often matter, it's the quantity that counts.

What else is there?

There is the sparse sparkle of television. Zap! BBC 1. Ugly-natured Cockneys screaming at each other. Zap! BBC 2. Englishman commentates breathlessly as a pair of turtles copulate. He hasn't been this worked up since private school. Zap! 'S' TV. English lads out on the town in a part of Spain I feel incandescent with pity for. The lads fight, molest girls and – how hilarious – flash their bare arses at the cameras. No discernible difference from their faces. Zap! Channel 4. English businessman, boasting about how much money he makes, recalls the day 'pooh people' took to the streets to protest 'sumfink or uvva' and he and his colleagues spent the afternoon photocopying £100 notes and letting the papers drift down onto the 'revolting plebs, *huh-huh-huh*'. Zap! Channel 5. Don't care about us in this part of the country – or don't realize we exist – and so we get no signal. They're doing us a favour. Zap! At last, something relaxing. A beautiful nighttime blizzard.

On the odd day when rain isn't strafing the window

like warfilm gunfire, I just stare outside, though I would rather hang myself by the privates than become a typical *Leòdhasach* curtaintwitcher. There's a story – if it isn't true then it ought to be – of some nosybastard from Ness who was forever glued to his living-room window, scrutinizing every detail of village life, day and night. He had everyone figured out – always nosy-parkering, always knew where someone was going, sometimes even before they themselves knew. One Christmas, a couple of the villagers got together and sarcastically (this is very *Leòdhasach*, too) bought him a telescope. Plus, of course, one of those brutally cooree* Christmas cards with a wishy-washy Old Testament picture and a black funereal text about loving thy neighbour.

So next day – Boxing Day – when *Niseachs*† are all burping into their *guga*‡ sandwiches or whatever, one of the villagers has had one elephant's skinful of whisky too many and he's staggering down the road like he spent the night inside a washing machine on a typhoon-struck ship. Now, the nosybastard is naturally perched by his window and he spies the pishtup guy from some distance.

---

* Cooree: Stornowegian. From the Gaelic *'cùram'*, this word is often used pejoratively. It usually implies something or someone is suffocatingly religious.

† *Niseachs*: Stornowegianized Gaelic. A *Niseach* is a native of Ness, a port in the far north of Lewis.

‡ *Guga*: Gaelic. A solan goose (a bird that thinks it's a fish).

He reckons the greyheaded drunk in the distance looks just like one of the local church elders. The thought of this sparks his, uh, native inquisitiveness, and he grabs at the new telescope excitedly, raises it to his eye and hastily extends it . . . thereby, in his sly agitation, smashing it right through his own living-room fucking window. Genius. You couldn't make this shit up.

Yep. Lord knows, it's the secular parables that have real relevance.

This island, though. I mean, perceptive ignorance is still ignorance. It was evenings of solitude and drink and shivering peatfires that helped me understand that if all these telescope jabberers would swap windowtime for mirrortime the Island might indeed be a less self-righteous place.

There is to the Island a mean-spirited greyness that is reflected in the skies above and the general outlook within, sourly possessive as the dull of thinking can be about their version of God. Every Sabbath when certain stunted individuals herd into pre-church gossiping congregations they are as cruel, petty and vindictive as children, delighting in misery, in other people's frailties. *Did*

Circebost: *the uncontrollable wish you sometimes have that you could live in a cartoon world – unpancake yourself after a safe has fallen on your head, walk off cliffs and defy gravity until you notice you're in mid-air, survive a fall of any height with a brief dusting afterwards, etc. Christ, how I wish I wish I wish I lived in a cartoon world where life is colourful and death is negotiable.*

you hear, they hiss-whisper in tingling abhorrence, *that the Marag's* son was done for drink-driving again?*

I always said he'd come to no good that one. And the sister's no better. Her time is coming, you mark my words.

Well, wasn't her great-great-grandfather just the same?

Trouble, the lot of them.

Always were and always will be.

And what about Jessie-Mary's girl, the crosseyed one?

Aye, her with the Catholic eyes, always crossing themselves. In the family way, and her just turned fifteen.

There was always something funny about her.

Oh she was like the rest of them, not quite right in the head. Giving crosseyed people a bad name, just.

And who on earth's the father? He must have something wrong with his own eyes.

Did you no hear about what happened when she went to the doctor's?

*Marag: Gaelic. A nickname. It's common in Gaeldom for people to have nicknames whether they like it or not. Many of the names in this book are nicknames. Karen Neònach = (in Gaelic) *'caran neònach'* = (in English) 'a little bit strange', etc. *'Marag'* means 'black pudding'. Stornoway is famous for its black puddings, although not among vegetarians.

Cradhlastadh: *the practice – a requirement in children and students of other languages – of looking up dirty words in the dictionary. Any practice that mixes mental edification and a sense of spurious thrill. (Heh, heh, heh, there's a river in Nicaragua called Pis Pis River. There's a place in Russia called Vagina; it might be amusing to go there, if you are female, and send a postcard to a would-be suitor, stating with sly subtlety 'Wish you were here'.)*

No?

Didn't the doctor say to her, And do you know who the father is? And she turned to him, bold as brass with her one eye going out for the shopping while the other one's coming back with it and she says, as true as I'm standing here, No. Who?

I do not want to live like this, under the control of one of those Churches that want to lead us not into temptation but into biblical times, into backwardness. I like living in the here and now because that's the only place I *can* be. I like temptation. Food tempts me and drink tempts me and *without them I would not survive*. These grey little Holier-than-Christ men would set the angels themselves fighting duels. I will not view the world through the Wee Free's* morose-tinted spectacles.

The Wee Free mind is often wee, but it's seldom free. This is not to say I don't admire their tenacity – that's what faith is, supreme tenacity. But I do not believe a God who created passion and compassion, rain and rainbows, stars and starfish, is sullen and unforgiving. On the absolute fucking contrary, I admire his style. For he also, I confess with a little admiration, created the likes of me. Mavericks, like his son.

Yeah, I love whatever creator naturally created artists and I ain't ashamed to say so.

---

* Wee Free: denotes the Free Presbyterian Church. The Wee Frees are God's chosen ones, if God is indeed as miserable as they believe.

My reasoning goes like this: if our *creator created us* in *his image*, then surely we ought to be *creative*.

Thus, the Island's God – who is, to so many, a mercifully spiteful, wrathful and vindictive god – made of me an Artist.

I built upon my Godgiven gifts. If my eyes are intense nowadays – and by fuck they are – it's because I've intensified my whole self: countenance, assertion, hairstyle, clothing, ongoing declaration of identity – hell, every outward and inward manifestation of me-ness made more fully me, me to the power of me, selflessly, to the greater good of Art. Only after BigBanging my ego, godlike, could I create my own art, something worthwhile. I've allowed myself to believe in myself. Only now can I embrace life and art fully, honestly.

God has the greatest sense of humour in the universe (cf. your sexual organs, the purposes plural they serve) and it is my Christian fucking duty to have a sense of humour too. Praise the good, nay, the hilarious Lord and this epitome-of-sour-gloom island he has created, to which I and my kind must be the new Elect, the teasing jokers in his pack.

I've made art out of the quintessential absurdities of this divinely mundane place. My objective, through art, is to escape the film-set and leap with a cry of triumph into the Actual. Cue God's admiring applause.

Small things, like levelling arrogant bureaucrats (always embittered English monoglots) with an introductory yarn

in Gaelic. Their looks of incomprehension, embarrassment or arrogance are my favourite Polaroids.

And as for my schooling in art . . . I remember fucking
up the requisite (who decided these were requisite?)
pencil drawings of a sheep's skull we had to do in 'art'
class. Jesus Christ, everyone without exception who ever
went to the Niccy had to waste half a term drawing a
fucking sheep's skull. Now, while I'm chuffed to fucking
smithereens Snuggles the Ram from Garryvard has been
repeatedly immortalized, one has to wonder about the
imagination of the people who teach – or even *call* – this
'art'. They're no doubt very lovely people with shiny
white and toothily yellow skulls of their own, so I'll give
them the benefit of the charitous here . . .

Did the Heads of Art (whose skulls, come to think of,
I'd like to X-ray and overwrite in permanent ink: 'If you
don't make wholehearted use of this free and precious
life, what good does it do to possess a human body?') –
did they have a cunning ploy? Were we all part of a
Warholian experiment of theirs? Did they make many
thousands of attractively garish primary-coloured repro-
ductions of these sheepskull pictures, which now sell in,
say, Japan, for hospital-sized prices?

I hope so, because – thus – redemption of sorts.

Listen, I have a recurring dream. Kind of a Grim

Crosbost: *the grey feeling that, as you get older, it seems every second
person you hear about or read about is no longer living. Ergo, your time is
drawing near. Nearer. Nearer.*

Reaper thing. Not the Grim Reaper as in the taxi driver we know as the Grim Reaper because his gaunt form appears in pub doorways after closing time and, with a nod of his head, a saddened drinker or two gets up and silently follows him into the darkness. No, this dream involves an actual Grim Reaper.

A skeleton, dressed in a hooded, billowy cloak, wafts through the huge fullmoonlit night with a gleaming scythe in his bony clutch. He's grinning, like all skeletons, but thoughtfully, not like all skeletons. He looks anxious. Mr Death has something on his mind. What the fuck, I wonder in my sleep, does Death have to worry about? (Fucking *taxes*?) Somehow, like an email you send by accident, he registers this thought of mine and next thing he's hovering like a suffocating blanket over my house. Death, drawing near. Then I wake up, panting, in a cold, oily sweat. Thirsty.

Something about this dream has sent a little depth charge sinking dismally in my mind:

I'll die young,

won't I?

So one day, down the Bràigh, sitting watching the

Dailbeag: *the realization that, with a few billion people on the globe, it's almost a certainty that at least one other person does some or all of the weird private mental stuff that you do.*

Dailmòr: *the subsequent realization that, in any case, many people reading of such weird stuff will, whether they like it or not, find themselves indulging in your strange behaviour at least once. Like telling someone not to think of a plane made of red candy-floss drifting overhead. And they do.*

waves as they snuffle and dribble around the rocks, crinkle and smoothe like laughter lines, Joe Idea, responding to my unburdening of this dream, gets out his flick knife and carves a pseudo-voodoo image of me into a slender piece of driftwood. He gets up and plants the stick figure in the sand. We're laughing as the gurgling waves lick over the stickman figure and Joe Idea makes up a nasty (there's no swearing like Gaelic swearing) incantation in the form of a Gaelic curse.

Three weeks later I very nearly drown in the infamous Drunken Coves' Midnight Butterfly Swimming Race in a slow, heavy sea at Cliff Beach, despite my being – excuse the departure from modesty here – a damn fucking powerful swimmer.

'*Am fear dhan chroich, cha d'tèid gu bràth a bhàthadh,*'* Joe says afterwards, not a trace of worry evident in his demeanour, countenance, or fucking seemingly ironed-flat forehead.

I reply as evenly as I can, a wee bit fazed but mostly just adrenalized by the whole thing, 'Yeah. But even the strongest man who was born to drown will drown in a half-filled glass.'

There's nothing to intensify your artistic determination like almost exiting the world via a voodoo driftwood stickman.

---

* *Am fear dhan chroich, cha d'tèid gu bràth a bhàthadh*: a Gaelic saying. 'The man whose fate is to hang will never drown.'

It was art, too, the first time we filmed. You know, Lewis is some – ahem – fucking landscape. We filmed Cailleach na Mòintich* from Cnoc na Tùirse,† the hill by the Callanish Stones. As all *Leòdhasaich* and a few bongilees‡ know, seen from a certain angle at Callanish, these hills – Cailleach na Mòintich – to the south form the shape of a naked woman lying on her back. Joe Idea and I made a stop-frame film a few years ago that shows the moon rising from her womb. We ad-libbed an appropriate commentary – part new-age bongilee bullshit, part filth, and it's got the potential to be an arthouse hit, a masterpiece for druidic and pretentious wankers alike. (Incidentally, what kind of ancestors did we have if the best pornography they could come up with was – let's call it a pornorama – a pornorama of suggestive hills? *Hoi, Cove, check it out – those hills over there look like a blone lying starkers on her back. Let's camp here a while, an erect some stones just to pass the time an keep the gaffers happy.*)

(Again, though, I mean *fuck*, this is the stuff, the art,

---

* Cailleach na Mòintich: Gaelic. Literally 'the Old Woman of the Moor'.
† Cnoc na Tùirse: Gaelic. Literally 'the Hill of Mourning'.
‡ Bongilee: ? A word of uncertain derivation, but common in many parts of the Highlands. Denotes a person – either weirdly bearded or glaringly rainbow-skirted – who moves to the Highlands to open an overpriced craftshop-cum-café that will also provide workshops such as 'Getting in Touch with Your Inner Fairy', 'How to Knit Your Own Soul', 'Highland Stone Circles – Learn How King Arthur and the Aliens Built Them From Magic Moondust'. Fuck, I'm not perfect, but these people are tragic – and they are *multiplying*. Be afraid. Be very afraid.

that would be Turner Prize-worthy if we were pretentious Southerners.)

What would it be like to live in days when art meant fulfilling a prestigious social need, and not just providing toilet paper to an onanistic élite? Now we have blue-eyed brown-nosed, double-figure-IQ'd, knuckle-dragging, mouth-breathing English Radio One DJs and Mid-Atlantic Ken and Barbies (who ought really to be *in* the Mid-Atlantic) doing our non-thinking for us, harbouring delusions of adequacy.

Cèilidh-time

A deranged wind has staggered across the Minch; it collapses over Lewis, screaming and keening and tearing at the houses from all sides. Indifferent black clouds taxi their cargo of ghostily uplifted seawater, drop it off into the demented wind. The walls groan and tremble as all the Cleared Highland townships would if ghosts really existed.

The coves – Jimmy the Tongue, Dead Geoff and myself – have congregated at my house with a view to bombing it out the Pentland Road in Dead Geoff's pickup truck for some peaceful loch-fishing. This was Dead Geoff's idea. Dead Geoff loves nature – inscrutably so, since nature has not been kind to him. Poor Dead Geoff; he has one of those Tupperware haircuts you hoped had died out in the seventies. I'm not saying he's slow-witted . . . but watching him get a joke is like watching a photograph develop in a film tray.

The Force Ten from Hell has taken us by surprise – a rare occurrence as most bornandbredandbuttered *Leòdhasaich* can tell the day's weather by glancing enigmatically at the sky. That 'if you don't like the weather, wait ten minutes' crap the tourist industry likes to preach just doesn't work. The weather works to its own rhythms, rhythms you can learn and respect if you know a place well. But, like a good idea, this storm has come out of nowhere, hit us hard and changed our plans. The sky is asserting itself, deepening from an ominous marble, Free Church grey, to something darker.

We debate our options. Staying in at my place is not one of them; Joe Idea (currently in bed recuperating) had been round the night before and we'd polished off all the whisky, rum and wine I'd had. (All necessary for one of those putting-the-world-to-rights talks where next morning you remember no more than that you solved all the universe's mysteries. What the answers are you no longer recall. That's why you drink again, in order to retrieve them. Solutions to the world's problems, you kid yourself, are important.)

'Let's go over,' I suddenly announce, 'to Captain Moses' place!'

'Ah, superb fucking idea, man! 'S been ages since we had a cèilidh over there,' Jimmy the Tongue says with a grin. He adds (superfluously), 'We'll stop off at the Trader for a carryout on the way over.'

Dead Geoff speedboats his pickup through slashing horizontal rain to the Trading Post where we get a quiveringly ambitious carryout. We then screech and skid our way up to the Cearns – Stornoway's puny effort

at a Bronx – where the hero known as Captain Moses
. . . 'lives' isn't the right word. *Survives*.

Captain Moses is a legend in Lewis and sundry ports
throughout the world. He's visited most of the world's
broken-up islands at one time or another and has the
elevated stories and the whipping wit-wisdom of the
typical *Leòdhasach* globalvillager. He's travelled to more
places than you can find on a map.

We hammer at the door, desperate as the drowning
men we half feel like. Captain Moses swings the door
open on us. As soon as he sees us, his eyes crinkle. You
have to love the Captain. His wild wintryClisham* head.
His hair a sparse calligraphy of branches drifting over the
craggy lit-moon of his face. Bigbooted and slim as a
tarasgair,† he is surely one of the hardest (drinking, working) men this sturdy slowseasonal island has known. His
voice has the quiet liltingly metallic quality of most
Leòdhasach men. His brine-fed days at sea have left him
with a thirst that God's own rum couldn't quench. His
eyes – you understand it straight away – have weathered
unmentionable storms. But when he sees the carryout
his eyes not so much light up as practically blind themselves. 'Get your arses in here. A few of the old codgers
are here too. Boys, we're in for a night of it!'

When I was a child I was lucky enough to spend a lot

---

* The Clisham: the island of Harris's Mount Fuji.
† *Tarasgair*: Gaelic. Peat-cutting iron.

of time in the Captain's company. 'There's many things I don't understand,' the Captain would declare, pulling on his poaching uniform in front of a Clearance-huge fire. 'But salmon isn't one of them . . . and the salmon is the wisest creature on this earth.' He would give a sooty chuckle and lounge out the door into the night. 'Help yourself to anything. And don't forget to go home.'

The Captain also has the Lewis obsession of attending funerals. Funerals. Funerals. Funerals. Friends, distant relatives (he had no near relatives – these would be eighth cousins twice removed, people he'd never spoken to), people he'd known fifty years ago, vague acquaintances – all deserve 'Respect. You have to pay your Respects.' Many times I heard this mantra as I watched him, red-eyed, ironing drunken creases into his churchwhite shirt. Yet whenever he raised the shirt from the iron's hiss to put it on, it was always ice-cream smooth. His tall, pinsmart figure attended every funeral that Respect demanded, irrespective of hangovers. 'But let the Devil himself,' Moses would announce with rumfuelled

Drinisiader: *the realization that some stuff you do is just plain weird, e.g., you watch a Korean film and ponder that, very possibly, there are bits of dog digesting inside that actor's stomach.*

Eòropaidh: *the niggling feeling (usually justified) that the person beside you (on the tube, bus, etc.) is reading your newspaper on the sly.*

Fionnsbagh: *the way some albums from your teenage music collection grow bland or raucous over the years so* Hey! Your parents were right. *And if they were right about that, they might have been right about other things too. Distressing.*

passion, 'bugger me raw with his trident if I ever get the *cùram*.'*

His religion is the unwritten scripture of the *beul-aithris*,† the stories and the songs that grew up resolutely from the unforgiving Lewis soil. I'd like to write more about this, but just buy me a drink one day and I'll tell you about it instead.

We follow Captain Moses' tidily shuffling body through the tatty hallway. He looks like he's a youthful hundred and twenty but is rumoured to be no more than eighty. I often wonder if those stories are true about some alkies being able to live for so long because their insides are so pickled they self-preserve, y'know, like the *Sasannachs'*‡ Queen Mother. As a sailor Captain Moses was credibly said to have won drinking competitions in which other competitors had died, self-poisoned.

A few of Captain Moses' cronies sit rosily by the fire. They turn to us and nod.

Fearchar the Corncrake is here, all bone and no meat, so skinny he doesn't cast a shadow. His head supports a shock of grey hair, not white and Godlike as Captain

---

* *Cùram*: Gaelic. To get the *cùram* is to become preciously and intolerantly religious in a 'the Old Testament was a good start, but it didn't go far enough' sense.

† *Beul-aithris*: Gaelic. The oral tradition.

‡ *Sasannach*: Gaelic. An English person. Interesting to note that the word in Gaelic has no pejorative connotations, though such often exists when the word is used as a loan word in English!

Moses' hair is, but deceitfully dignified-looking all the same. His complexion is bad, a lifelong acne and booze victim. He recently attempted to snog – fuckit, molest isn't too strong a word – molest a good friend of mine. When he sees me tonight his face is redder than a communist who's embarrassed after lazing about in the sun too long. We always like to warn Fearchar not to stand still at street corners cos drivers frequently come to a halt thinking he's a traffic light. We like him zero out of ten. He lies like a cheap watch. His ex-wife – a fine doorful of a woman – is the only person I've ever known who went deaf *voluntarily*. I owe Fearchar something unpleasant on my friend's behalf. I wish for the ten millionth time that I enjoyed, or could even tolerate, violence. I'm a fuck-up when it comes to being anything other than peaceful. (So to speak. I mean, self-destruction doesn't count, obviously.) I can't even watch boxing on telly. It's like a venomous ballet, gorillas doing speeded-up t'ai chi, apple-fisted morons with teeth for brains punch splatter punch splatter kill kill.

I nod. 'How's it going, Fearchar?' Hopefully you've not got much longer to live.

He raises a glass with a sad smile. 'Ach, getting there.' And downs it.

Johnny Banana is here. A ratlike, pin-eyed man, skin

Gearraidh-bhàird: *the late January realization that, instead of bolstering your dignity, your New Year resolutions have broken you and robbed you of it.*

like puked-up porridge, and a head that's small and balder than a snooker ball; he's quite a kindly person, though. His wiry body is slumped like a piece of string in the armchair, as though he has no muscles. Yes he fucking does. A drunken Glaswegian once said to him in the Clachan, 'Hey, pal. Is it no a fuckin tragedy? Ye spent all that time washin and combin yer hair an then ye fur-goat tae bring it wi ye.' Among Johnny Banana's friends, this was the verbal equivalent of throwing up in a swimming pool. Johnny B took the guy outside for a wee chat. That Glaswegian extended his holiday in Lewis from a casual drinking weekend to nine bedridden days, what with him being a wee bit broken up in hospital and all. We like Johnny Banana eight out of ten. His favourite phrase to use in pubs is '. . . unless you want my fist for lunch.' He saved me from a beating once when I got on the wrong side of somebody. Well, I got on the wrong side of somebody's boot.

I nod. 'How're you doing, Johnny? Good to see you, man.'

'Awfurfuck'ssakesit'syourselfman,' he grins. ''S been too long.' He winks. 'We'll have a good night the night.'

Murdani Nardini is here. His large-set body dominates the comfiest chair in the house, the one nearest the fire. He wears – as usual – heavy black glasses and a heavier black moustache, one which seemingly prevents him from smiling. He's the Godfather of a powerful clan within the Gaelic Mafia. He's used to people feeding his ego when his ego should be on a diet. The Gaelic Mafia is a touchy subject in Lewis. Outwith the Highlands it is said: 'The Gaelic Mafia made me an offer I couldn't . . . understand.'

Whether it was an ironic or a threatening gesture I don't know, but at least one of Murdani's former business acquaintances woke up one morning to find a sheep's head sharing his pillow. (Story goes, the guy'd been on the booze and at first thought it was his wife, but I don't believe that part; let's just say the guy who told me it is well versed in the art of bovine scatology.)

Being a *duine dèante** in the Gaelic Mafia, Nardini is often seen on Gaelic TV programmes pontificating vehemently about the language. To be honest, he's one of those three dozen rentagaelicgobs whom I can't look at in real life without seeing a stream of subtitles flashing across his chest. We like him two out of ten, and that two isn't liking, it's amiable intimidation. He's wearing a brown paisley-patterned shirt with three buttons open to show off his vaguely hairy chest and a medallion (what is it? a gold medal from the *Mòd*?),† and he's in a pair of tight silky trousers and a wig, neither of which fit him size- or age-wise. In some cases, the ignorant people

---

* *Duine dèante*: Gaelic. A made man.
† *Mòd*: Gaelic. A national Gaelic gathering that celebrates – competitively – such arts as song, storytelling, poetry and having a good time. Usually referred to in English – not without some justification – as The Whisky Olympics.

are right and Gaelic money does have a lot to answer for.

I nod, muster all my deadpanicity. 'You're looking good, Murdani.'

'*Och, feumaidh tu do dhìcheal a dhèanamh,*'* he replies, to remind me that he speaks Gaelic. He gives my blue, older-than-the-Bible *geansaidh*† and faded-near-to-nothingness-and-held-together-with-patches jeans the once-over. Eilidh designed the patches and sewed them on for me. Murdani eyes them with disdain. The patches say, in lush purple swirls, 'All fur coats are stolen' and, in blood-red slashes, 'I read banned books' and, in simple black newstype, 'Fuck You. Too much is not enough.'

'*Feumaidh, a Mhaighstir Nardini, feumaidh,*'‡ I reply blithely.

'Close the world's eyelids, *a bhalaich,*'¶ Captain Moses says to me.

---

* *Och, feumaidh tu do dhìcheal a dhèanamh*: Gaelic. 'Och, you have to do your best.'

† *Geansaidh*: Gaelic. Jumper, or, if you're of that persuasion, sweater.

‡ *Feumaidh, a Mhaighstir Nardini, feumaidh*: Gaelic. 'You have to, Mister Nardini, you have to.'

¶ *A bhalaich*: Gaelic. Boy (vocative). Often used affectionately or playfully; the person need not actually still be a boy.

Griais: *when your finger automatically presses 9 before dialling a telephone number from home. A classic sign of* griaiseachd *– that is, you are spending too much time in the office. (When someone told you to go out and get a proper job you should never have done it. Why did you do it? Your life is slipping away.)*

I duly cross the room, my shoes stickily snogged at by the carpet as I go. This is the house that launched a thousand parties; a huge number of people have ended up in this house who have no idea they were ever here.

I pause at the window. The wind and rain are so violent now it's like the house is being rammed through a car wash. I snap the curtains shut with a shiver and turn back to the here-we-go.

'Oh, here,' I say to Captain Moses, handing him a bottle of rum. 'And there's a wee bit more.' I indicate the bags of booze that dangle clinkingly from Jimmy the Tongue and Dead Geoff's hands.

I flop down into the empty chair and the others sit on the floor. Dead Geoff trembles in the shadows, hiding from the attention as is his way. Shame. There's a great fire blazing away like madness.

Dead Geoff has never had a girlfriend, though there is a murky rumour about a prostitute in Inverness, which I hope for both their sakes is not true. My mission is to try and get Dead Geoff a life, but I've been trying to do that on and off since we were fifteen. Might as well

Griomsiadar: *when the stranger sitting next to you on the bus/plane/ train falls asleep, a complex multi-faceted pretence, called* griomsiadar *comes about. It is difficult to explain, but it involves one of you trying to ease the other one off your shoulder, one waking up amid a pretence that he (it is always a he) wasn't snoring. Or indeed, sleeping in the first place. So where did the fucking drool on my shoulder come from? The whole thing is one long fucking embarrassment. So we pretend it isn't.*

perform a séance with a monopoly board. Fucking *tru-aghan*.* Still, I love an underdog, even when it's Dead Geoff, whose greatest aspiration in life is to be promoted to underdog. Dead Geoff might have the intellectual vigour of a decomposing sloth, but I will always defend The Underdog – comes with being Scottish (and being a bit fucktup myself).

Captain Moses makes a show, standing before the roaring gelly,† of unscrewing the cap off the bottle of Trawler. He then drops it to the floor, mangles it with a terrific bootstamping and mutters slowly, drily, 'Och, well, dammit! I suppose there's nothing for it now but to finish the blasted bottle.'

Cheers all round.

Fearchar the Corncrake is excited. He screeches, 'Drink up, ya fuckers, it's cèilidh time!'

It is.

And we do.

A true cèilidh is not – and never was – a polite gathering of immaculately dressed Gaels and pseudo-Gaels sipping

---

* *Truaghan*: Gaelic. A pitiful person.
† Gelly: Stornowegian. A fire, usually a good (big) one.
Làcasdail: *you've started telling a filthy joke to your friends, who are hanging grinningly on to your every word, when your mother (father/ grandparent/minister/priest/local fucking do-gooder) walks into the room and makes full eye contact with you. That blushing hesitation – you're on the very verge of the punchline and your friends are desperate to hear it: do you carry on? I don't know – but I do know that the Gaelic word for this situation is* làcasdail.

at malt whiskies while applauding on cue a set menu of drawing-room-influenced *clàrsach** plinky-plonks, melodious bagpipe caterwauling, loathsome reels, agonized lovestruck *cailleachs*† and young Gaelic divas mourning the loss of the waulking.‡ A true cèilidh is a group of friends coming together round a warm fire and sharing in that warmth, actual and spiritual. The warmth of the hearth and the more important warmth of the human. Fuck pseudo-sentiment, in other words, and bravo and long live real feelings of camaraderie.

We're grateful for the blazing fire Captain Moses and the others have built up, but the collective stenchcloud that rises visibly above Jimmy, Dead Geoff and me as our damp *geansaidh*s dry on our bodies brings to my mind images of rotten seagulls, dead men's socks, Satan's armpits on a Sunday, when Hell is at its hottest. Had we actually gone out fishing we'd probably have come back smelling better.

---

* *Clàrsach*: Gaelic. A harp.
† *Cailleachs*: Stornowegianized Gaelic. Old women.
‡ Waulking: i.e. of cloth, sometimes referred to as fulling.
Lingreabhagh: *any jokey bigotry that is actually dangerous e.g. in parts of Africa many impoverished people used to refer to AIDS as American Ideas Discouraging Sex. The disarming realization that humour can be dangerous.*
Losgantir: *as the telephone rings and you're (for example) drying your hands or putting your clothes on, 'Hang on! I'm coming!' you shout to the phone. The belief that somehow the phone will understand this and ring less piercingly;* sin agad losgantir.

'Well, well,' says old Captain Moses, shaking his head at the fireplace. 'There are nights the waves want sky, all right. There are nights the waves want sky.' He has this tattooed on his chest, and when he gets drunk enough he shows it and tells the story behind it, which involves, if I recall, a hurricane, a mermaid (or vision thereof), a hospital in Galveston, an angel (or vision thereof), and a medical certificate he demanded from a doctor to prove that he was clinically dead for a time. Captain Moses stands by the fire, occasionally leaning on the mantelpiece. He never sits down, not even in pubs. He has a theory that if he sits down he'll get drunk.

'There are that,' mutters Johnny Banana, 'there are that. Hoi!' He shouts at no one and everyone, the way you do at a cèilidh, 'Do yous not remember what happened to Big Barney the Glaoic's* boat the last time the wind was like this?'

There are sufficient low nodding murmurs to indicate that everyone present is well aware of the story, but at a cèilidh, of course, that doesn't matter. Half of the story

* *Glaoic*: Gaelic. Idiot. Moron. (Face it, we all know the feeling.)
Marbhaig: *a typing error, the consequences of which could be grave, e.g., instead of 'doing', 'dying'. Lapsus calami, but with an element of morbidity.*
Mealabost: *the practice of inventing futures for yourself (e.g., gold medal iceskater who redefines the rules / attitudes – you know the kind of thing I mean.)*
Mealabost eile: *the sure knowledge that such a future will never come to pass and never would in an infinity of possible universes.*

is in the anticipation. It was oral traditions such as ours that invented people like Alfred Hitchcock before they invented themselves.

'Aye,' says Johnny Banana, settling back into the telling of it. 'It was a wind like tonight's, that came from nowhere, a wind that was so strong it blew the tattoos off Loose Lucy's arms. Who knows where they are now – for all I know, they probably landed on some poor bugger's face in Honolulu.'

Everyone laughs at the right places and we all pass a bottle round with a smooth and practised preciousness, like a baton.

After one round it will be finished, and another bottle already on its way. On we go.

'Anyway,' Johnny Banana resumes, 'this story's about Big Barney the Glaoic, whom we all know and love as a man so lacking in the upstairs department that his only useful period of employment was as a scarecrow.'

Mùirneag: *life's multitudinous, let's just fucking call them flies, this dictionary compiling is hard work – anyway, things in life that distract you and soon make you forget that urgently seeking the meaning of life's essence was a thought – indeed a priority – in the first place. What's on telly tonight?*

Pàbail: *the feeling you get when driving through a thoroughly remote rural area (e.g., parts of the Highlands) and you see a solitary house, countless lonely miles from the nearest neighbouring house and you wonder just who lives there and how they occupy their time.*

Pàbail larach: *the same question, but applied to a densely populated city (e.g., 'Birmingham – who in the* hell *would want to live there?')*

'Yeah,' I interject, 'the last time Big Barney did any work he was trying to get out of his mother.'

'Aye,' adds the Captain, 'and he'd still be there now if there hadn't been someone there to give him a hand.'

(Fantastically, it *is* true that Barney worked as a scarecrow – for a month. Better still, he was actually *sacked* (for falling asleep on the job, presumably drunk). Apparently a horizontal scarecrow is less effective. Sometimes I love this island purely for its narrative potential. Only fucking trouble is, everyone thinks it's fiction.)

'The respected Mr Glaoic took it upon himself to visit his boat during this storm – he says now, to check up on the boat, but we all know that he was planning to go out fishing in a wind that would have sent the *QE*2 somersaulting. Anyway, he goes down to where his boat is moored and – it's not there. No blooming *sgeul** of it at all. He goes home and cries and bawls all night, lamenting his lost boat and hence his lost livelihood, which in any case was singular only in that fish – of, it's reputed, a higher intelligence than Signor Glaoic himself

---

* *Sgeul*: Gaelic. In this context, sign.

Suainebost: *the feeling that even the most passionately xenophilic world-citizen has that, with the best will in the world, some languages are just plain ugly. And yes, that most certainly includes German, a language in which 'My love is like a red, red rose' sounds like the slobbering growls of a senile Doberman.*

Suardail: *the word for a celebrity whom you none the less (despite their fame, wealth etc.) feel you could genuinely bond with over a drink, e.g., Sean Connery, Wynona Ryder, Ewan McGregor, Claire Danes.*

– that these fish knew that a pleasant swim around his boat was just about the safest thing any rightminded fish could do.

'Next morning, the storm had upped and vanished to cause chaos elsewhere. Myself and some of the men went down to the shore and there, sitting on the beach, loaded to the gills with shingle and stones, is the Glaoic's boat. The wind had only whipped enough rocks into the boat to weigh it down, push it down under the water, and hence *save* it from the storm! Which only goes to show you can keep a boat, but not a fool, down!'

We all express our rumheightened appreciation of the story.

'Hey, Captain,' I say, 'why don't you tell us the Lewisest Story that Ever Came Out of Lewis?'

'Oh yeah,' The Tongue exclaims, 'the World's Greatest Small Town Story, a classic.'

But Moses, standing solid and hunched by the fire, shakes his head. 'Not tonight, boys.'

Cèilidh etiquette has it that you don't force someone to do something if they don't feel sufficiently comfortable (drunk). Unfortunately, it also means you don't stop someone who is too drunk from embarrassing himself either – a song with lyrics that collapse in on themselves seconds before the singer does, a fiddler who doesn't realize his fiddle is back to front, that kind of thing. It's all been seen and done before.

I resolve here and now to write a play based around a

cèilidh in which the audience all get a dram* on the way in, and they have to participate, providing their own songs and stories too. It should go on all night and the actors would have to sign a medical certificate absolving me of any responsibility towards damage to their health resulting from the play. I store the idea in the back of my mind, determined to work it into something special one day. The story of the play would be partly improvised each night according to the locality and the audience's contributions. I could involve a few artist friends who are anything but shy, make something special out of this . . .

Moses, seeing that Fearchar the Corncrake is itching to sing, suddenly invites Dead Geoff to take a turn.

Everyone knows Dead Geoff's only party piece is . . . too rude to mention here. He has a contortionist's ability to . . . Jesus, I can't even mention it. Think of the most disgusting thing you can think of, think of a lifeless guy named Geoff doing it bucknaked right in front of you, think of him actually eating the cucumber afterwards, and wonder to God why this guy isn't making a living out in Bangkok where respectable businessmen pay top dollar to see this kind of filth. I've always been too scared to search for any Internet pages Dead Geoff might have created. He's jobless, spends a lot of time in his bedroom, and he must have *some* way of making an income to pay for his drink and smokes.

---

* Dram: a measure (invariably too small) of whisky.

Dead Geoff wearily gets to his feet, sloughs his clothes, and performs his mercifully indescribable thing. The ensuing applause sounds paltry, but that is because everyone is usually too astonished to concentrate enough to clap. Usually it's less the sound of a few hands clapping than the thud-thud-thuds of jaw after jaw hitting the floor. Dead Geoff accepts his applause with accustomed good humour, and sinks down with relief into his semi-anonymous shadow. The more I think of it, the more I suspect he's either a secret dot.com millionaire or imminent prison fodder.

Suddenly Fearchar the Corncrake exclaims, 'Hey, I'll tell my joke!'

It's an old joke, but we let him, since it's really a cue to let Johnny Banana do one of his party pieces.

Fearchar stands up, spreads his arms, clears his throat and declares, minister-pompously:

In the beginning, the Good Lord Our Father, seated upon His throne on high, turned to the Archangel Gabriel and remarked, 'Gabe, I'm going to create Scotland today. I shall make it a country of beautiful, inspiring mountains, purple glens, and rich green forest. I shall give it clear, swift-flowing rivers and I shall fill them with salmon and trout. Where the land is not mountainous it shall be lush and fertile, and the people will grow barley on this land and create from it an amber nectar that shall be much in demand all over My world. Underneath

*the land I shall cause there to be rich seams of coal. In
the waters around this country's shores there shall be
an abundance of fish and beneath the sea I shall deposit
great quantities of oil and gas . . .'*

*'I do beg Thy pardon, Sire,' interrupted the Archangel
Gabriel, 'dost not Thou think Thou art being rather too
generous to these Scots?'*

*'Think so?' sayeth the Lord with a righteous smirk.
'Wait until you see their neighbours.'*

We appreciate the joke, but now it's Johnny Banana's
turn to dazzle us with a poem, unique, melodic, anonymous, marvellously cadenced.

'Ach, yous know what I'll be doing now. It's what I
call the "Neighbours We Could Have Had" poem. Or,
welcome to Scotland, welcome to Lewis, the good people
of . . .'

He takes a deep breath. We all do.

And he starts to chant. (You should try chanting this
too, especially if you're in a public place.)

'. . . Afghanistan, the Republic of Albania, the Democratic and Popular Republic of Algeria, the Principality
of Andorra, the Republic of Angola, Antigua and Barbuda,
the Argentine Republic, the Republic of Armenia, Australia, the Republic of Austria, the Republic of Azerbaijan,
the Bahamas, the State of Bahrain, the People's Republic
of Bangladesh, Barbados, the Republic of Belarus, the
Kingdom of Belgium, Belize, the Republic of Benin, the

Kingdom of Bhutan, the Republic of Bolivia, Bosnia and Herzegovina, the Republic of Botswana, the Federative Republic of Brazil, Negara Brunei Darussalam, the Republic of Bulgaria, Burkina Faso, the Union of Burma, the Republic of Burundi, the Kingdom of Cambodia, the Republic of Cameroon, Canada, the Republic of Cape Verde, the Central African Republic, the Republic of Chad, the Republic of Chile, the People's Republic of China, the Republic of Colombia, the Federal Islamic Republic of the Comoros, the Democratic Republic of the Congo, the Republic of Costa Rica, the Republic of Côte d'Ivoire, the Republic of Croatia, the Republic of Cuba, the Republic of Cyprus, the Czech Republic, the Kingdom of Denmark, the Republic of Djibouti, Dominica, the Dominican Republic, the Republic of Ecuador, the Arab Republic of Egypt, the Republic of El Salvador, the Republic of Equatorial Guinea, the State of Eritrea, the Republic of Estonia, the Federal Democratic Republic of Ethiopia, the Republic of the Fiji Islands, the Republic of Finland, the French Republic, the Gabonese Republic, the Republic of The Gambia, the Republic of Georgia, the Federal Republic of Germany, the Republic of Ghana, the Hellenic Republic, Grenada, the Republic of Guatemala, the Republic of Guinea, the Republic of Guinea-Bissau, the Co-operative Republic of Guyana, the Republic of Haiti, the Holy See, the Republic of Honduras, the Republic of Hungary, the Republic of Iceland, the Republic of India, the Republic of Indonesia, the Islamic Republic of Iran, the Republic of Iraq, the Republic of Ireland, the State of Israel, the Italian Republic, Jamaica, Japan, the Hashemite Kingdom of Jordan, the Republic of Kazakhstan, the Republic of Kenya, the Republic of Kiribati, the Democratic People's Republic of Korea, the Republic of Korea, the State of Kuwait, the Kyrgyz Republic, the Lao People's Democratic Republic, the Republic of Latvia, the Lebanese Republic, the Kingdom of Lesotho, the Republic of Liberia, the Great Socialist People's Libyan Arabic Jamahiriya, the Principality of Liechtenstein, the Republic of Lithuania, the Grand Duchy of Luxembourg, the Former Yugoslav Republic of Macedonia, the Republic of Madagascar, the Republic of Malawi, Malaysia, the Republic of Maldives, the Republic of Mali, the Republic of Malta, the Republic of the Marshall Islands, the Islamic Republic of Mauritania, the Republic of Mauritius, the United Mexican States, the Federated States of Micronesia, the Republic of Moldova, the Principality of Monaco, Mongolia, the Kingdom of Morocco, the Republic of Mozambique, the Republic of Namibia, the Republic of Nauru, the Kingdom of Nepal, the Kingdom of the Netherlands, New Zealand, the Republic of Nicaragua, the Republic of Niger, the Federal Republic of Nigeria, the Kingdom of Norway, the Sultanate of Oman, the Islamic Republic of Pakistan, the Republic of Palau, the Republic of Panama, the Independent State of Papua New Guinea, the Republic of Paraguay, the Republic of Peru, the

Republic of the Philippines, the Republic of Poland, the Portuguese Republic, the State of Qatar, Romania, the Russian Federation, the Rwandese Republic, the Federation of Saint Kitts and Nevis, Saint Lucia, Saint Vincent and the Grenadines, the Independent State of Samoa, the Republic of San Marino, the Democratic Republic of Sao Tome and Principe, the Kingdom of Saudi Arabia, the Republic of Senegal, the Republic of Seychelles, the Republic of Sierra Leone, the Republic of Singapore, the Slovak Republic, the Republic of Slovenia, the Solomon Islands, Somalia, the Republic of South Africa, the Kingdom of Spain, the Democratic Socialist Republic of Sri Lanka, the Republic of the Sudan, the Republic of Surinam, the Kingdom of Swaziland, the Kingdom of Sweden, the Swiss Confederation, the Syrian Arab Republic, the Republic of Tajikistan, the United Republic of Tanzania, the Kingdom of Thailand, Tibet, the Togolese Republic, the Kingdom of Tonga, the Republic of Trinidad and Tobago, the Republic of Tunisia, the Republic of Turkey, Turkmenistan, Tuvalu, the Republic of Uganda, the Ukraine, the United Arab Emirates, the United States of America, the Oriental Republic of Uruguay, the Republic of Uzbekistan, the Republic of Vanuatu, the Bolivarian Republic of Venezuela, the Socialist Republic of Vietnam, Wales, the Republic of Yemen, the Federal Republic of Yugoslavia, the Republic of Zambia and the Republic of Zimbabwe.

'A toast – neighbours we could have had!'

We raise a drink, down it, then applaud long and hard. No one else I know can do Johnny Banana's party piece. It's easy to forget what a miraculous planet we live on, to ignore the magic of naming things, to overlook our place in the overall scheme. I always consider Johnny's performance a piece of art to be proud of and I wish for the umpteenandahalfth time he'd let me film it.

Christ, I have a lump in my throat, a stupid dampness in my eyes. I nod my head solidly, hold Johnny's gaze. And grin. 'Sheer fucking poetry. It's a beautiful world.'

Then, breaking the spell, Murdani Nardini decides it's his turn to entertain us. Johnny Banana's always a hard act to follow, but when Murdani Nardini talks, everyone listens. I have a secret little game I play when he's talking. It's called 'Count the Clichés', but I'm going to leave the rules of it wrapped in mystery.

(Murdani despises the police. Once he took me for a drive around the lunar landscape of Harris. He was looking for a place to site a luxury home he'll never own. (Of course, this was before the police took away his driving licence on the grounds that it didn't exist.) I paid no attention to what he was saying – I just sat there counting the clichés and marvelling that his stories were up to twenty miles long in the rain.)

'This is a true story,' Murdani growls, 'and it only happened last month, you see, and what it was was, the top brass at the Cop Shop were up in arms because the boys in blue up here were too busy playing at Hamish

MacBeth and not making nearly enough arrests. They were told to shape up or ship out, pronto. So what do the pride of the constabulary do when they need to make enough arrests in the Highlands for a pat on the head and a good report card? Right. Drink-driving. Talk about barrels, fish and shooting.

'So the élite of Highland law enforcement heard that there was going to be a big wedding on down at the Harris Hotel. They duly go down there in their cop-mobile, survey with satisfaction the large quantity of cars parked outside and, judging by the uproar from within the hotel, the large quantity of whisky being consumed inside. They rub their hands with glee, and wait.

'The first guy comes out of the hotel and to say that he's paralytic is an insult to self-respecting paralytic drunks everywhere. I mean, this guy can barely crawl, never mind walk. And right enough, he eventually makes it up to a car, drops his keys a half-dozen times or so, climbs in, starts up the engine and drives off.

'Well, the cops are overjoyed. This guy is *nicked*! They chase after him, blue lights flashing and blaring. But the guy – the guy doesn't stop. Doesn't even slow down. The cops are thinking – this guy's either so plastered he doesn't care, or so drunk he can't even see. They're beeping their horn, flashing the headlights, calling out with a loudspeaker – anything to get the guy's attention, to get him to pull over.

'They might as well not exist. He's driving on and on

over the winding Harris roads, without a care in the world.

'Finally – oh, must be an hour and a half later, as if just noticing them, the guy pulls over into a layby.

'The cops pull up behind him and leap out of the car, a bit like Starsky and Hutch, had Starsky and Hutch been a coupla shaved apes but with less class. "Outta the car!" they yell to the poor guy.

'He obediently gets out of the car. The cops ask him to do a breath test and, to their surprise, he agrees amiably enough. Blows into the bag.

'Result: a very definite negative. Not a trace of alcohol in his blood. The cops look at each other, confused, which is easily done.

'"Well, officers," says the guy, "it's conclusive. I'm the decoy."

'Meanwhile, all the genuine drink-drivers have driven home unimpeded.'

Everyone laughs heartily, slaps their thighs and wipes the tears of mirth from their eyes, complimenting the Godfather on his ability to tell such a wonderful and, clearly, authentic story.

'Now wasn't that just the Big Ben of all wind-ups,' bellows Fearchar the Corncrake. 'Well, now,' he continues, 'how about a song?'

'Aye,' I interject, ' "*Hi Ro Hai Ro Caite Bheil Mo Giro?*" '*

* '*Hi Ro Hai Ro Caite Bheil Mo Giro?*': Stornowegianized Gaelic (song). 'Hi Ro Hai Ro Where Is My Giro?'

Fearchar ignores me. '*"A Ribhinn Og"*,* I think.'

Now Fearchar's voice is the proverbial bum note in the music of what happens; it is to the average voice what the tractor is to the flute.

'Isn't it enough,' I shout, 'having one howling gale outside, without another howling Gael inside?'

Everyone guffaws at that and Fearchar scowlingly takes his seat.

'How about instead,' says old Johnny Banana in his measured tones, 'something from the man of the house? How about it, Captain?'

Everyone turns to Captain Moses, who has been unusually quiet all night.

The wind outside rages, the fire's crackling light spits long shadows gesturing around us.

Captain Moses takes a pull at a bottle of rum.

'The one story,' he says, with a dark blaze in his eyes, 'that's been on my mind lately is this one.' He pauses, takes another swig. 'The true story of the owl and the pussycat.'

* *'A Ribhinn Og'*: a wonderful Gaelic song, frequently murdered by people who shouldn't drink, people who shouldn't sing, or people who simply just *shouldn't*.
BTW, I think I've given you enough new Gaelic words to learn. Hopefully now you've developed a strong urge to learn the language. Go on! Do it! You'll be amazed! The language has only eighteen letters in its alphabet! Each letter is intimately connected to a tree! There are so many amazing aspects to learn about the language while you're learning the language that you'll never be bored.

For one moment the room's oxygen is sucked out and replaced with incomprehension. I give a curious look at the bottle in my hand and I'm about to pinch myself when Moses chortles, eyes twinkling like the harbour lights.

'Ya fucking eejits. The story is, of course, the Lewisest Story Ever to Come From Lewis. Also known as the World's Greatest Small Town Story. Or, as the ministers know it, the Ultimate Parochial Story. It's a true story, I swear that on my dear mother's grave. I know it because I was there. A true story, all right. More than one man I've knocked stone cold who didn't believe it.'

None of us doubts it: the story or the knockouts. We glance at each other, delighted. None of us, I believe, ever gets tired of hearing this story.

'It was a night much like this one,' Captain Moses begins, 'only maybe not quite so wild. Wild enough, though. The rain was beating at the window and no one wanted to be outside. Our own house was full. And not just because of the weather. Why, then?

'Because this was the twentieth of July 1969 and all the inhabitants of all the civilized nations on Planet Earth wanted to be near a TV to watch Neil Armstrong, who had Scottish ancestors, become the first human being to set foot on the moon.

'All our neighbours were round. My mother, God rest her soul, was still with us. She was in her eighties then and her best friend was there too. We'll call her Mrs

Muffin, though you all know her real name. Mrs Muffin was the minister's wife and she was really a kind-hearted soul. The wife hadn't yet left me, plus we had all manner of neighbours and friends and family round. There were about forty of us crowded into the living room. Christ, looking back on it I should have been selling tickets.

'Anyway, everyone sat or crouched or stood where they could, except for my dear old mother and Mrs Muffin and me; we had the couch in front of the telly. My wife – the ex – ex-human being I call her – the ex-wife was pouring cups of tea and passing round the home-baking and I was sneaking a snifter or two from a flask of the good stuff. Everyone was in fine fettle, and there was the TV with all the tension building up, the old black-and-white TV, the only one on the street in them days, which is why everyone was at our place.

'Well, one of my neighbours was old Bert MacDonald. Bert Einstein, we used to call him. A real boffin, with the huge egghead and the sellotaped spectacles and everything. Always had his nose in a science book, always out in his shed, which was next to mine. I'd be out there having a fly drink and I'd hear him building a time machine or whatever he was working on. Nice enough guy; I had a lot of interesting conversations with old Bert though I never knew to this day what in the hell he was talking about. Gravity this, relativity that. Told him I'd enough problems with my relatives without him adding to them. Ol' Bert's been dead twenty years now, and he's probably still arguing with God that he doesn't exist.

'Anyhow, back to the story. Ol' Bert Einstein is going on about all the marvels of technology they've created to get that rocket up there into space and everyone's nodding cos they've never even heard of a quarter of the words he's using. But mostly we're all glued to that old black-and-white TV set. A spaceship, from earth to the moon. Imagine!

'And Bert says, and I swear the old codger had a tear in his eye, "I wish it was me going up there. One day it'll be as easy going to the moon as taking the ferry to the mainland. I was born too soon. I wish I'd been born thirty years later."

' "Well," says Mrs Muffin, "Going as far as Inverness is good enough for me. I just thank my lucky stars it's not me that's going up there."

' "You're not exactly spaceman material, I don't think, Mrs Muffin," I says.

' "And that's just as well," Mrs Muffin says in her lah-de-dah voice. "I've never been off the ground higher than the Reverend Muffin's pulpit. And that's quite high enough for me. I do suffer from vertigo so."

'Well, the tension is building up on the TV and the wind and rain outside are battering at the window, when Mrs Muffin says, "No, but seriously, it's a brave, brave thing those men are doing and my prayers are with them.

' "Going all that way," she says, "and on a night like this."

'And that, my friends, says as much about Lewis as any story I've heard.'

You have to love Captain Moses. We laugh ourselves stupid. Drink ourselves stupider. It's how we cope.

Doll-Sized Grave

Meanwhile I'm sleeping a lot (despite rough, kaleido-scopic nightmaring), going for moody, filmic walks by the sea or ambling swan-necked through Stornoway's gawking streets, meeting pseudo-friends in the Caley for whiskies or actual friends in the Coffee Pot for breaks-from-whiskies, and all this while naturally falling head-over heels in lust every thirty seconds. And – fucking weird – hugging people for the first time in my life. I mean, I'm experiencing something like selfless love. That's when I first understand something is wrong. It's like the love a six-year-old feels for a pony. Everyday moments have me brimming over with an ugly happy-sad gooeyness. (Examples: a little girl playing with toys in Woolies, even a young couple heading out to the Castle Grounds arminarm with a carryout). Maybe it's no more than post-youthful fucking morbidity, maybe alcohol can trig-ger a fucking one-man renaissance, I dunno. But some-thing has catalysed this internal hugfestival out of the messy whateverstuff that more or less holds me together inside. And, since I don't understand it, I don't like it.

Daytime, I wander round hugging my 'Hello's and 'Hey's and *'Sin thu fhèin*'s and *'Dè tha dol?*'s* to everyone I half know, and all my 'Cheerio's and 'Seeya's and *'Cheers an-dràsda ma-tha*'s.† I wonder if I'm having some sort of breakdown; this outburst of love for humanity is so far outwith my me-ness I begin to fret. I mean, thoughts of love – it ain't lust – hit me like trains, one after another. The thousands of poets in history who've written elegies: didn't one of them stop to realize that what they were doing, what they were writing, was too late?

(Am I elegizing, prematurely-but-only-just, my own demise and the death-rattles of my culture, my language?

Do I, after all, *care*?)

Death is fucking with me, I know that much. Every night, that leering skeleton appears in my dreams, maybe just hovering in the corner, sometimes even in pleasant-ish dreams, as predictable as an artist's signature. I dream I can see and read tiny, vivid-coloured texts within my bones, the DNA of my body's unswayable novel. The story of me is looking none too fucking hilarious. I see teeth jagged like broken bottles snuffling along the floor towards me, I feel minuscule black butterflies fluttering poisonously around my nostrils and ears, I plunge from graceful breaststroking skyswims on to hungry, hagfaced, tree-sized mushrooms.

---

* *'Dè tha dol?*'s: Gaelic. 'What's doing?'s.
† *'Cheers an-dràsda ma-tha*'s: Gaelic. 'Cheers just now then's.

I frighten at the thought of falling asleep, half-convinced I won't wake up. I try to think of people I'd hugged that day, but all I hear is whining *Leòdhasach* voices gossiping my disappointments, my failures, my hypocrisy.

People stare at me in the street as if they've heard some viciously delicious gossip about me. This is the *Leòdhasach* way. I keep trying to cheer myself up by remembering the Lewisest Story that Ever Came Out of Lewis. Maybe there'll be a cèilidh again soon, and I can lose myself in stories like that one, the familiar pure-grade bullshit, the top-quality stuff that touches and convinces and makes you greet with manly laughter after a few hard drams.

One night Eilidh phones to tell me that Fuzzy – her gorgeous wee shitebag of a cat – has died, fucking tractormashed, and the news sends me into a manic half-hour of crying and howling, literally howling, at the nightsky. Then an emptiness of peace settles over me. I'm not reacting to life like me. Who the fuck am I? Who decided I can't be who I've always felt I should have been? And – uh, has there been a marble spillage?

The day after Eilidh phoned with the news we go to the shop where she works and get a cardboard box that had housed tins of Fuzzy's favourite cat food. His coffin. Eilidh has bought a plastic toy tractor – a big one – from Woolies and we ritually smash it up with a sledge-hammer, then pour its remains into the box on top of the gawky pulp that is what's left of Fuzzy. It's a still day, windless and almost respectfully silent. Eilidh has written a tinywee poem on the ping-pong ball that was Fuzzy's favourite toy and she drops it into the box, refusing to let me see it. But the ball bounces off a plastic shard from the tractor and poings out and onto the ground. We both inadvertently erupt a 'we-shouldn't laugh' sort of snigger, more like a sneeze. I respect Eilidh too much to pick up the ping-pong ball, both of us knowing my curiosity would force me to read what she's written. She bends down for it, returns it more carefully to the box.

I've dug a deep hole in her back garden – thirsty work but it's amazing the driving strength whisky gives you. I've also – it felt properly improper – poured a little libation into the mouth of the earth for reasons more personal to me than the cat, I suppose, but at least I'm seeing him off with a valued possession.

Eilidh places the box – you can tell it weighs pathetically fuckall – into the ground and says a silent prayer to an animal heaven that makes my head spin to think about, like when you try to consider before you were born (remember what sensations you had?).

The thought breaks over me. Didn't I kind of *love* that cat? All those times, crashed out on Eilidh's sofa, I would waken with a weight on my chest, fuzzily thinking my heart was giving up its token effort, only to stare into a struggling drowsiness in the eyelids of that cute little greeneyed furball, his august paws stretched out in front like a cuddly wee sphinx. How when I'd eat crisps he'd lick my fingers with a tiny ticklish rasp, then stramash the crispbag through the cottage. If he'd ever met a real mouse he'd have been pissed off it wasn't cheese-and-onion flavoured. How I'd lower a cereal bowl down to him, let him lap up the pool of Alpeny milk. 'That's your lot, Fuzz.' I'd stroke his bib and he'd purr seductively, licking his lips. All those ragatag wrestling bouts we had, his tight claws and sharp wee teeth often winning against my skinny hands and determination not to hurt him in the tiniest amount. He once – accidentally overzealous – tore a strip from my index finger that kept me away from the guitar for a month.

I hug Eilidh. Her body is shaking so I hug her tighter and warmer until she gentles. Then I set to overearthing Fuzzy's cardboard coffin. I've slept on the streets in foreign cities, I've been mugged of all my busking money in more places than I can remember, I've woken up in hospital palpitating like my heart's drinkbattered muscle was racing me to death. But shovelling the earth over that stupid fucking coffin is one of the hardest things I've ever done. By far.

I take some serious pulls at the litre of chicken just to keep going.

Finally, I heap up the huge spoon of the shovel and dollop the last of the soft earth onto his doll-sized grave.

'Let's do the wooden cross now,' Eilidh mumbles lifelessly.

The world pauses.

And buckles.

A warm splash falls from my eyes and lands on my right hand – on a thin red scratch, a light, free-running scar like a child would make on paper with her first crayon. A scar I kind of wish will never heal.

'You get on with that,' I mutter, and clear my throat badly. 'I gotta go.'

Tears, like tiny slivers of vodka.

I turn away.

Blind My Eyes, Insist I'm Handsome

One thing almost as bad as drink-driving is drink-dreaming. Those who don't believe me haven't a scooby because they haven't experienced it. I swear by all that is holy and all that is not, I cross my imminently heart-attacking heart and hope not to die, that the following is true; the worst thing in this life I have experienced is a drunk dream. Because a drunk dream is more real than the real.

What's horrific about it is that you believe the dream is real for as long as it lasts. For *at least* that long. A drunk dream is a dream that's supervivid, a cross between a film and a short story; it has backstory and understanding, subtlety and immediacy, yet it will not depart from you for reasons that leave you feeling nastily meaningful.

Fuck, I don't want to write this, but I have to.

A thousand times or so I've woken from the sinking smells of my couch, or bed if I made it that far, to realize that something has happened and it's taken me the best part of the day to realize it was only a dream, an intense, drink-boosted dream. Even the good ones are bad. All they have in common is that they were more real than the real. We have a saying in Gaelic: *Chan eil ach rabhadh gun fhuasgladh ann am bruadar na h-oidhche.** Or, as Henry Havelock Ellis put it, 'Dreams are real as long as they last. Can we say more of life?'

I have this tremendous illuminating dream that stays with me all the time and I need to write it here, because it still hurts. If you've held these pages – these pages which I sometimes think of as my hands – if you've held these pages in your hands – all the way up till now, then you'll maybe understand.

I'm going to leave you in a dream that had all the detail of a short story and all the realism of a film – rather, all the realism of reality. I swear it happened exactly as I've written it here. I leave you, then, temporarily, where the drink left me . . .

*   *   *

Eilidh bursts into tears.

Her heart, a water balloon, is pricked: it overflows with pang after pang of pitifilled love.

'Oh my beautiful, hurting baby.

'Trobhad, a ghràidh.† *Come on now, darling. It upsets Mummy*

---

* *Chan eil ach rabhadh gun fhuasgladh ann am bruadar na h-oidhche*: Gaelic. The dream of the night is but a warning unsolved.
† *Trobhad, a ghràidh*: Gaelic. Come here, darling.

to see you upset. If you cry, I cry – you know that. Fuzzy, a ghràidh,* let's not cry.'

As usual, Eilidh's a useless mother.

'Isd, a ghràidh.† Let's not cry.'

It does no good.

Fuzzy's green eyes float in fat, wobbly tears, his little breast puffs up and down like a frog's, his voice is a strangled mangle of sobs and snorts.

Fuzzy is a grey cat with a human child's face, mewling, red-cheeked, crying.

'Crying doesn't help, a ghràidh,' Eilidh pleads, knowing that she is lying. Why is she lying? Everyone feels better after a good cry. At seven years old, Fuzzy knows to trust his instincts more than his mother's words.

She knows Fuzzy doesn't cry on a whim. He was five when his father died, so he's learned what crying for real is. He cried so much after Jake's death that she thought his eyes would be ruined, but she was too nervous to take him to a doctor with a reason that sounded insane when voiced aloud: 'Well, Doctor, I'm afraid he's cried so much he'll end up blind soon.'

Her poor, hurt baby. Now he's crying again.

'Isd, a ghràidh, isd.'

Time, darkly bland as ever, passes.

Like a hearse in a sunny street.

Fuzzy quietens; there is a terrible, stifling silence.

Those tears trembling and rivering and steadily slowdiving down

---

* *A ghràidh*: Gaelic. Darling (vocative).
† *Isd, a ghràidh*: Gaelic. Quiet, darling.

onto his tiny paws are ghosts of the tears he lost for his father. But they are also a warning.

Miles away, out at sea somewhere, a storm rolls and breaks.

Eilidh covers her eyes with her hands.

Jake was unique, like getting a grown-up's present for your thirteenth birthday, a godsend; that's probably why he had to die.

A summer's morning, with Jake walking beside her on the moor. Suddenly he grabbed her and pushed her down to the earth. There, thrust down into the spongy heather, she was taken irreversibly, like destiny, like a little red boat in a high storm, like a painter ripping through a vital, paint-thirsty canvas, like a song of wild glee at a funeral, like something unearthly; her insides loosed red tears of angry joy. Afterwards, Jake had looked deep into her eyes, he had seemed to melt into her weakened eyes, and he'd cried out softly, 'Oh, a ghràidh, how happy I am. How truly fucking happy I am.'

Those obsessive, passionate months. Those long hours of breathlessness and chatter and revealing of secrets. Caresses ached for. Tears. Tears that were easily kissed away.

Could she really expect to know that twice in one lifetime?

She wants to be given and she wants to be taken.

She wants someone to drink her to the final dregs.

Sudden, soft and warm – a delicate breath on her lips. Who . . . ?

It is Fuzzy. He says nothing, he doesn't need to. He touches his cheek to hers, all calm now and porcelain and chaste. He presses his head close to hers and she feels gently, immediately *more real than she has felt in months. Fuzzy smells of heathery playfulness and his raw, animal breath.*

She wants to hug him to pieces.

And then jigsaw him back together again.

She throws love letters onto the peat fire. They burn with the smell of pubs, whisky and smoke. She almost believed in God. Jake must have burned with a poet's intensity when he wrote them. The words are filthy with white heat and red. She floods, she drenches when she reads them. Now she is burning them and the heat blasts at her hands and face, but it is not at all the rough heat of the words he wrote. She doesn't feel this heat any more than she would feel a flitting shadow. The darkness in the room lengthens and then shortens again, thickens and shrinks. Everything in the room seems to be continually changing its size and shape. Her mind feels elastic, removable, worn.

She wants to burn with them. She should have died first. She wishes Fuzzy would kill her. Accidentally. He is young. The young have innocence punched into their DNA. He is young enough to kill her utterly and get away with it, unhindered even as an anchor-shaped cloud. Maybe she should start hitting the bottle and spliffs again, since she had only meant to give them up for Fuzzy's squatting time in her stupid womb. Her womb is like a padded cell people go to when she's half asleep.

She should burn the Bible. Is it a sin to burn the Bible if you don't believe in it? What if she burns the Bible and finds

Jake's filthy letters made whole again tomorrow, resurrected like the Nazarene?

She watches her love life burn.

She has been ploughed hard.

She is a failure of self-esteem. The doctor told her that. 'It seems to me,' he said, looking over his fat red spectacles, 'that yours is a failure of self-esteem.'

He put her in hospital, a pure, white prison.

A smug man with a Satanic beard pushed her and all the other women down into their tears. She would have preferred her head down a toilet. He grinned like a politician. He told them he was satisfied by their tears: she's to suppose they passed that test.

There was Art Therapy with Miss Plum, who was a delirious, twiggy little woman who could not stop smiling and nodding. Maybe what she really wanted was to teach retarded children. Her coos of admiration rose on cue like the doves people release at charity concerts, the ones that choke in urban pollution. Every day she flounced into the room giggling and handing out crayons like childhood treats.

With a violent passion, Eilidh submitted: daffy drawings of houses soon became lightning-struck brothels. All men grew horns. Miss Plum drowned her in praise. Eilidh battered modelling clay into demonic Cupids with arrows for penises. Miss Plum was demented with pride. She helped persuade them to release Eilidh. Miss Plum gave Eilidh her phone number, which she blackened with crayon, tore into confetti, and burned with a curse.

'Mummy,' says Fuzzy.

'Yes, a ghràidh?'

'Why are we going to bake a cake at midnight?'

'Everywhy.' It's a word her father had used and she hates it. She hates herself for using it.

'But I don't understand,' Fuzzy falters anxiously.

'Today would have been Daddy's birthday. Don't you want to help Mummy bake a cake for Daddy?'

'It's just that things have . . . have been strange again these days. And I don't like it. Mummy, I'm scared.'

So is Eilidh, but she knows better than to tell Fuzzy. 'Be a brave wee puddy-cat. Be Mummy's baby.'

'Am I still your baby?' he exclaims, as if hardly believing his ears.

'Of course you are, a ghràidh. You're Mummy's one and only special baby and that's why Mummy loves you so much. And that's why you have to trust Mummy.'

'Oh, Mummy, MUMMY!' Fuzzy purrs, his little paws clinging to her leg like a trap. 'Oh, Mummy, I don't care if it is midnight, you're the best mummy in the world and I want to bake a cake. I do! What kind of cake will we make?'

'Well, what kind do you want to make?'

'Chocolate!'

'Double chocolate – Daddy's favourite! The best kind of

cake!' Eilidh detaches her leg from Fuzzy's embrace and glances towards the kitchen. 'We'd better go into the kitchen and start making it.'

In the kitchen she leaves the light off, to make it more secret. Greyish rain falls on the windowpane, half-heartedly. A little moonlight seeps through and casts a pale foundation over Fuzzy's eager face.

While Fuzzy looks out, ears cocked, at the night, Eilidh turns the gas on. It hisses like a filthy whisper in her ear.

'Mummy, I know where the Plough is.'

'Where is it, a ghràidh?'

'It's there.' He raises a paw. 'No, over there. Look where I'm pointing.'

'Oh, yes.'

'You're not looking properly. It's over there, where Daddy's star is, remember?'

'Of – of course I remember. Daddy's watching over us all the time. Wave at him.'

'Hello, Daddy,' he says, pawing at space, but she detects a note of uncertainty in his voice, like when he's not sure about Santa.

Eilidh has closed the kitchen door.

'Mummy, why are you putting towels under the door?'

'Because, a ghràidh, it's draughty and a gust of cold air will spoil the cake. This is Mummy's secret special recipe.'

His forehead crinkles tinily. 'But the air won't get in – Mummy, why's the oven door open? It stinks, it stinks in here.'

'Come here,' she says, and Fuzzy looks a bit wildeyed but

Eilidh kneels down with her arms open and she is offering a Big Mummy Hug and Fuzzy moves openly towards her and she holds him tight, she buries her face in his little coat and she covers her eyes with her hair and she holds on to his little body for dear life.

★   ★   ★

And God help me, I wake up cold in sweating sheets, knowing it means something, even though cats can't talk, even though Eilidh once had a miscarriage but has never had a child, even though Eilidh has never had a boyfriend called Jake, far less one who died, even though Eilidh is one of the least suicidal people I know, even though this and even though that, I know it, I know it means something, just you see if I'm right, oh fuck, you see if I'm right.

Being a Loner Is a Lonely, Lonely Business

I'm a loner, the kind who pretty much can't stand his own fucking company. Despite my hugging people like it's going out of fashion, you can't deny that most people are predictable and this depresses me more, maybe, than anything else, because it's so constant. I mean, people are so addicted to routine on this godforsaken island, they get suspicious of the slightest change. Lewis is the kind of place where everyone knows not only who everyone else is (for twelve generations) but also where they're going and why (this also applies to the dead).

   – Oh, but Effie, it's Thursday, it's *my* turn to pay for the scones.

   – Nothing fresh, man, you've seen it all.

   – Och, just a pint of the usual.

   – Same old same old.

   – Ach, why change the habits of a lifetime?

   – Wouldn't want it any other way.

   – You can always trust the tried and tested.

   – If it ain't broke, don't fix it.

   – Don't upset the applecart.

– Oh, but Agnes, no, Agnes, no, it's Friday, it's *my* turn to pay for the scones.

Ad nauseam, ad mortem.

One of my favourite Lewis quotations came from two soft old *cailleachs** (one female, one male) gossiping in the Coffee Pot. Sweetie-wife number two (the guy) shakes his head and tut-tuts fruitily. 'Aye. The brains were putting him daft, he was that clever.'

Fucking gossip! Mouth-to-mouth recitation. The negative that's first developed and then enlarged.

The main reason more people don't commit murders on this island is they're scared of what the neighbours would say. I swear, being banged up in a shitsplattered cell as Big Dave Skullcrusher's number one bitch is *nothing* compared to the ignominy of Aunty Murdina muttering acid 'I told you so's over the reincarnated-teabag tea and stodgy homemade pancakes.

I head for the Caley Public, where I order so many drinks that when Joe Idea almost instantaneously appears (he has a magical nose for free drinks) he assumes I've anticipated his arrival and have racked them up for his benefit.

'You should fucking market that nose,' I tell him.

He looks at me quizzically. 'Aye, well, whatever.'

You know, once upon a time I couldn't even go into a café on my own, never mind a pub: too exposing.

---

* *Cailleach*: Gaelic. An old woman.

What happened to that self-consciousness?

I had my first sip of alcohol when I was ten. Cider. Some friends from school and I found it stashed under a bush out the Castle Grounds. We were always exploring the Grounds in those days. Kids still go scrambling around there on their bikes, which makes me smile. Some continuity is good. One habit that has slightly eased, though, is the noble Lewis tradition of taking an underage carryout into the Castle Grounds, drinking it with a bunch of friends and having freedom and fun, stupid glorious energetic fucking fun, all the better because it's illegal. Nowadays spy cameras dot and spot the woodlands like eyes on a peacock's tail.

That day, it was Kenny the Cleg who noticed the carrier bag. He did well to notice the carryout there, the Castle Grounds being so totally fucking clarted in litter back in those days. There were five of us, the raggle-taggle arse-end of a tyre-stealing gang. Every kid who lived in Stornoway back then belonged to a tyre-stealing gang, kind of a rite of passage. Nowadays they probably just go straight ahead and take the whole car but these tyres were for building the biggest gelly on Guy Fawkes' night. Gangs raided each other's tyres all the time. The most important thing in the world was getting a juggernaut tyre and a few mini tyres from the Battery Gang.

Back in our day, those tyre gangs were everything.

Blood was spilled.

Noses were burst.

Faces were pulped.

Toughs were sent to bed early.

Everyone but me tried the cider. They gagged as they sipped at it, but called me a coward and a chickenshit piece of chickenshit for not even trying it. 'Okay,' I snapped. 'Hand us the bag.' I pulled a can out of the wet, rustly carrier bag and snapped back the ring-pull as though I knew what I was doing. When I first tried coffee I spewed – knowing I'd no chance of making it to the toilet – right into the kitchen sink, dishes and all.

I put my lips to the tin, tilted my head back and let the piss-coloured stuff flow sweetly and poisonously into my mouth. It tasted of badtempered apples, like apples that had been liquidized up with petrol.

This is disgusting, I thought.

This is different, I thought. Dangerous.

The dark taste was doing funny things to my stomach and head.

Hmm.

This is bad, I thought. Really bad. I want more.

I had more.

Plenty more.

At first a feeling of buoyancy and ecstasy came over me like nothing else I had ever experienced outside of football; it was like scoring a goal with the whole school applauding and cheering, particularly teachers and girls, those lovely blossoming confident girls, but then everything tilted and I puked up all over myself and my bike, and the world dizzied and I fell down and I felt so weak and tearful I wanted to die.

Or, to put it another way, before everything tilted and I puked up all over myself and my bike, and the world dizzied and I fell down and I felt so weak and tearful I wanted to die, a feeling of buoyancy and ecstasy came over me like nothing else I had ever experienced outside of football and it was like scoring a goal with the whole school applauding and cheering, particularly teachers and girls, those lovely blossoming confident girls.

I had never felt so good.

Lovely alcohol. A new presence emerged from the bosom of everything. What had struck me most was the rightness, the familiarity of it. It was like bumping into a friend miles out on the bare moor when you were skiving off school. Understanding and recognition, a chemistry of rich subtlety. I don't know you, but we're friends. Bloodbrothers. I would do anything for you, and I expect you'd do anything for me.

This feeling of mutual need lasted for weeks, months, years. Reality took on the shifting, self-transforming quality of a dream. And because this sensation was so vibrant, so alive, it was more real than the sober mundane; drink showed me reality without its clothes on. The shared reality-landscape we inherit, I surmised, is a bluff, a prop. Fantastic how such realizations enrich a person's life.

Surely, I wasn't really alive before drink. I was escaping the film set, leaping with a cry of triumph towards God's admiring applause.

Fast-forward a few years. Like I said, I've got to suppose the intervening time between that formative cidery day out the Grounds and this evening in the Caley happened to me in real time but it sure didn't feel like it.

Here I am.

There Joe is.

Joe eyes the drinks ravenously. What are friends for? I am grudgingly happy to share . . .

After a few hours he vanishes in a drinksodden haze. Joe's a friend, and friends are like Gaelic proverbs: as often as not they go without saying.

I find myself chugchugchugalugging a pitcher of beer and blissfully floating into a Jacuzzi-like feeling of alcoholic saturation.

I'm getting to the place I want to be. Wilfully remote. Like an island.

But suddenly, before I can take any pre-emptive action, I'm being prattled at and smoked over by Golden Shower (don't ever call her that to her face). Golden Shower, in a beige and purple mini-dress, making not so much a fashion statement as a fashion punchline, is a woman of the world who once went out with a mild-mannered mate of mine. She gave him an education out by the Pentland Road that actually scared him off girls for eight and a half years. Anyway, she's a strong role model for people who like golden showers, and I'm sure she runs a support group and has a grand old time promoting yellowy weather everywhere. I'm a bit drunk.

'Dlkjfyar dlkjfayr dliry,' she says.

I let the words stream past my ears like tiny misguided darts.

'Idkjlfayr diuv aalk lkdcior,' she continues.

'What? Can't hear a word you're saying. I'll guess. The answer's no, not even if I had a concrete umbrella.'

A tinny version of Nirvana are playing 'Something in the Way' in the background. I want to listen, but she looks astonishingly hurt. She raises her tone. 'What the fuck are you on about? Why are you always so fucking hostile?'

'Cos I don't like people. C'mere. Give me a hug.' I try to pull her towards me, but she slaps my hand away. (I'm kind of glad then and – even more so – now).

'You're an angry little fucker, aren't you?'

'Just disifuckingllusioned. Buried a beautiful friend today.'

She looks at my drinks. There are rumours, I know. This is Stornoway, after all. She stares at my drinks with disgust, which is nice, what with her being nearly as drunk as I am. Her nose accordions in distaste. 'I hope that's not alcohol,' her wheedling voice says.

Without missing a beat I cast a baleful glare at her cigarette. 'I hope that's not carcinogenic.'

One all, right? Damn fucking right an I'm right. And I'll win this, easy.

She snorts. 'Is it true you're an alky?'

'Some people will believe anything if you tell them it's a rumour.'

'Sitting here at a bar without so much as looking at anyone. Where's the fun in sitting drinking alone?'

'Cos when I start talking to people I tend to talk such high-quality bullshit they don't understand or appreciate me.'

'Yeah, well, you've got a higher opinion of yourself than most other people do.'

'In the country of the blind, the hideous are handsome. And that's the other thing. When I talk to people, they unfortunately feel the need to respond.'

'How can you be an artist,' she scoffs, 'when you don't even take an interest in the people around you?'

I vaguely recall that she has/had aspirations to be an artist herself. 'Maybe I don't go around staring at people all the time. That's because I know the people here already. Better than I need to. I see very clearly that the people here are . . . *diminished*. Uh-huh, *so* fucking diminished they'd be better off dead.'

'You're supposed to be this artist and you don't even have an ounce of humanity for your own people. You make me, like, puke chunks.'

Somehow this riles me, but I'm too absorbed in my drink to get worked up. I speak calmly. 'I don't have an ounce of humanity for my people? I have a fucking life's worth of ambition and love for my people. And they're not *my* people. They don't belong to me. I gave up that right when someone decided I didn't belong to them. They're not my people and I'm not theirs.

'They don't understand me, I understand them all too well.'

'Listen to you, ya pompous prick. The Andy fucking Warhol of Stornoway. We should have a local holiday on your birthday.'

'I don't need birthdays and I don't need fame. Listen, this isn't an island, it's a fucking lifeboat. What I need, if I need anything, is for people to learn something from my art.'

'Arsehole.'

'Ah, forsooth. Much of obnoxion is there in the air.'

'You act like you're some bigshot famous artist. *Oooh, I've been around the world twice. I've been everywhere. I'm a big famous fucking artist.* When all you did was busk from one sorry little city to the next, prob'ly sleeping in a shitty old sleeping bag in seedy little parks. Artist, my arse. You were a fucking beggar, playing your guitar on the streets to beg money.'

'Nice mouth,' I remark. 'When does it shut?'

'A fucking no-good beggar. An artist who'll never even be good enough to be a has-been. A fucking *pseudo-eccentric.*'

She's still trying to get a rise out of me. She won't. 'Yap yap yap. There's fuckall pseudo about me.'

'With that many grudges you could open a chip shop on your shoulder.'

'I've always been this way. If you don't understand what I'm saying, I suggest you exercise your brain – it is, after all, the little things that count.'

'Yeah, well, I'd love to see things from your point of view but I'm afraid I can't get my head that far up my own arse. You're a lazy pretentious alcoholic fuckwitted failure. I can't believe where you got your ego from, since you've accomplished nothing but beg and busk like a million people, fucking hippies an all that, before you, on a world fucking egotrip. You make me sick!'

I burp, a thick acidic one. 'I make myself sick. So we've got something in common. Listen, trying to hurt me is as useful as putting a button on a sock. But this could be the start of a beautiful relationship. We could be lovesick.' I laugh at my crappy joke. 'Like lovesick teenagers. I puke in admiration of you.'

She looks into my eyes, almost curiously.

We fall quiet, listening to the waves of conversation and laughter crashing against all the drunken bodies wavering about the bar, the smoky air seeming to rush in and rush out of my ears like a bloodtide. We're submerged in it all. The huge grey smokiness like an eternal Lewis sky and the limpid murmur of the heart tap-tap-tapping at my chest. Inside, I'm all washed out, whisky-purged, numbed. Everything seems to pass through me with that same indifference the wind has with flags. I have little sense of who I am and what I'm doing in this pub. I cling giddily on to the suddenly recalled word *lovesick*.

'Let's go back to my place,' I say, 'and be lovesick together.'

She stops staring. Her lips slip open and her tongue emerges, tottering hesitantly, as if she is about to say something. No, that's not right. The movement's more carnal. The tongue sways hypnotically like the head of a snake. She suddenly grabs the back of my neck, zooms my head forward and kisses me gratingly on the lips and teeth.

A pushing.

An opening.

Our tongues thrashing like fish.

I taste blood.

She withdraws. 'All right,' she says defiantly. 'Your place it is.'

'Yeah,' I hear myself saying, 'my place it is. My place it is. My place in life it isn't. Ain't got no golden umbrellas. Just me and myself and I.'

I halfswoon off the barstool and find myself reeling away from her.

Her voice, jagged and threatening like a smashed beer bottle: 'Hey! Where – the – fuck – are – you – going?'

As I shove my way through the smoky, heaving throng, I hear her call me an asshole (when did she turn American? what happened to arsehole?), a fuckwit and a fucking loser (another Americanism – too much TV). I burp up stomach acid. There is a tight throbbing in my head.

In the fresh salt air, I lurch round onto Castle Street and stagger down towards the taxi rank. I need to be home. On my lonesome ownsome. God bless the homely dolour of a taxi.

There is a sad strange kitten-sized hole in my life no woman can fill.

Refreshed and Renewed as You Decay

Whatever else the fuck happens, time passes. I relax a little, mainly through avoiding human contact. I paint and read and build monstrous artefacts out of accumulated driftwood, which I then burn, mesmerized. It helps those internalized Damoclean clouds of Lewis disintegrate. I go out to buy food occasionally, but I've disconnected the phone and stopped watching TV; the world could have come to an end and I doubt I'd have really noticed or even cared all that much. I've lost a few pounds.

Even if I have little to do but attempt to make art mean something, I am alive at least. That much I understand. Surviving in a monotonous environment. Determined not to yield, but surviving. Sometimes Eilidh comes to the house, knocks, drums or kicks on the door, then flusters away as a disgusted note magic-carpets through the letterbox.

Spaceman!
    You fucker, I'm worried. Quit the Anne Frank act and get back into the real world.

A sharp slap across the face and lots of hugs,
Pink Panther

That kind of thing.

One day I wake up like I've been in a hole in the ground. I realize pretty soon that I'm okay; I've slept in holes in the ground and I know the wet earthy feeling leaves the head less contaminated than this.

No, it's just that the air in my bedroom is so stale it has given me a headache.

I open a window. Blue sky, light wind and creamy white clouds. The sun is daring to inject Lewis with sparks of warm carcinogenic happiness. Among the mildly scrolling clouds birds somersault, flap-happy hieroglyphics. I like them. Their music is profound and needy. Usually birds frighten me senseless, wheeling and falling and prodding and whooshing overhead like superior beings. These birds sound desperate, though, their songs are shrill, a skewed and acute mustering. A pure disharmony. Endearing. It's a song of need and I know about that.

Fine. I go out for a walk. It's actually hot, not just optimistically hot. Short dresses, pervy shades and stickily shared ice creams hot. God bless the rare days when the sun streams down on Stornoway like hot rain.

Sauntering down Island Road – it's cool, the way hot days make you walk more slowly, with a swagger – I see a beautiful young Japanese woman in slim and shapely white jeans and a blue cut-off top revealing a glittering belly piercing. A face to learn painting for. Two cultures, two strangers. I try to imagine our hearts are moving us closer, imperceptibly, as stars shift, or mist approaches. I yearn to taste of the – say, twenty-two, twenty-three – cherry trees of her life. A girl so perfectly beautiful I want to fall down on my knees and plead with her to understand that with beauty like hers must come responsibility. Innocently swaying through life, a girl can destroy countless men, men like me. Love is pain. (Ever wondered why it's called a crush?) Love kills. (Listen, if you don't believe me, pick up today's newspaper.)

A woman that beautiful throws the whole environment around her out of kilter. When she looks in the mirror is a woman like this astonished at her own beauty? I know I would be. One day men will invent a way of looking at beautiful women that shows them we don't mean to stare, we just can't help it. Eilidh once told me that the major difference between men and women is that if you go up to a stranger on the street and tell them their bum is too big and their hair looks stupid, if it's a guy he'll punch your face in but if it's a woman she'll burst into tears. Then again she also told me a story about a guy – we'll call him Tarquin since I hate that name – who used to hang around street corners in New York saying to every single woman who passed, 'Hey, lady, wanna kiss?' One day a guy goes up to Tarquin and says, 'Hey, buddy, I been walking this route the past month and every day I see you hanging around at this corner saying to every woman who goes past the same goddamn question – *Wanna kiss?* I just gotta ask, don't you get slapped around a lot?' 'Sure I do,' replies Tarquin. 'But I also get kissed a lot.'

This Japanese woman is such a vision of beauty and desire she will, I know, leave the rest of the day redundant, will leave time itself languishing around the duller heat of lesser beings. I want her to train those inkblack eyes on me so I can send her a telepathic message of sincerity and love. And of the shy truth: *I'm wounded. Take me away from here. Take me away from myself. Please, please fix me.*

Why can I only talk to women when I'm rubbery with drink?

She passes on, without noticing me, staring into an empty Hebridean heat, a tourist with all the self-absorption that a tourist automatically assumes, and I know I'll never see her again. This happens thousands, probably millions, of times an hour across the world. We should all learn something from this.

Buggered to fuck if I know what it is, though.

I suck in a huge lungful of air, hold it for four seconds, onethousand twothousand threethousand fourthousand, breathe out. Everything's loss anyway. I listen to the voices in my head.

– Cheer up, you fucking miserable *Leòdhasach*.

– I'm trying.

– Yeah. *Very.*

I *should* cheer up. It's a fittingly gorgeous time of day. Sometimes Lewis is a liberal place. It's the police who are uptight: the moral police. You forget that hateful baggage on a late morning such as this. The easy bustle of life slowed down by weather, warm sensual breezes, thoughts of lunch and the feeling that life can sometimes be good, even in this ordinarily grey and largely un-acknowledged part of the planet. It's all about learning how to let go. And appreciating things. Like drinking-in time.

Ah. Drinking-in time. As a lovely woman I once knew called it. In Spain, this was, a couple or three years ago-ish. Time for drinking in the sun and the breeze and the imminent pleasure of food and drinks and then siesta time. Which for me and her meant very little rest. I adored her English. 'I love you over the moon,' she used to say. *I la-av yoo ovar da moo-oon!* I pure fucking melted with that. Juanita E. G., where are you now? Mous-tachioed and married, according to The Tongue, who knows everything there is to know about women, even though he has never travelled further than Inverness in his life and he knows five women, mother and aunts included.

I think I know the you that you now are, Juanita. Some lucky *señor* has won your heart. He better be treating you right. You have one kid, with another on the way. You're both in love, still. Very much so. Your extended (and yet very close) family is your life. You soak in the cleansing therapy of mass as often as you can – two, three times a week. You enjoy hearty meals with radiant wines and laughter. Music. Happiness. Sun. Good health. Life is for enjoying. You still play the guitar. (Hey, Juanita, I still know the sad Spanish ballads you taught me even if I no longer play them: also the frenetic ones that hurtle along like kites dancing in the sky.) You never mention me to your husband, though he suspects there was a me at one time. Maybe he quietly seethes over his jealous image of me, a muscled Highland artist who lives for art and nature and honour, who lives a free and easy life of valour and dignity and loyalty.

If he only knew me for the fuckup I am. He would laugh. Or worse, shed a pitiful tear.

Juanita was poor and exquisite. I was poor and wine-smitten. And ever since those decadent Spanish days, I cannot imagine a late morning like this one without recalling drinking-in time, without recalling her, Juanita of the silk eyelashes and wine-red kisses.

That's how it is, I think, unloading a sigh as I wander along the claustrophobic part of Kenneth Street. A person's life is made up of episodes. Some long some short, some vague some vivid, like dreams. You just have to accept that. The various chapters that have been my life are not the harmonious blendings of a spectrum, like a great big family hug, such as well-balanced people experience. No. Mine is a jagged cardiograph, the raw tracings of a man with a damaged heart. That's why there's drink. It wipes the mind clean and speedily regulates the peaks and troughs.

Peaks and troughs.

Life is episode after episode of peaks and troughs. Despite politicians there are sunsets. Despite history there is tomorrow. Despite death there is uncertainty. Despite wage-slavery there is art. Despite loss there is sleep and time, both of which you can count on to refresh and renew you as you decay.

Heading up posh, flowery Scotland Street towards posher, austere Matheson Road I pass by a gangly twenty-something with a babyish weatherbeaten croft-spawned face. I have no idea who he is, but I know him at once. Left school with no worthwhile qualifications. Arsed about at school to please his pals, to disguise his insecurities. None too successful with the girls – too nervous, too self-conscious. At sixteen he was wangled a job driving a fork-lift in a warehouse, by his dad. Smokes like a kipper. Now he's doing a welding course at the college and hopes to make something of it. Gets fall-down drunk every Friday, every Saturday. Same pubs, same drinks, same faces.

Here he is. Face like a spat-out chewing gum. New York Yankees baseball cap, spray-on jeans and a hooded sweatshirt declaiming the might of a triggerhappy black Los Angeles gang. A true product of the times. Insular Lewis smotherhugged by global America. Black pudding meets black power. What the hell would the children be like? Tshust giv mee thuh fish an tships, muthurfuckur, or I'll bursht ya, man. Damn! What's a tshoochter* got to do in this town to get a bit of serviss around hee-ur? Tshust yoo wotsh it, cove, or I'm gonnuh bust a cap in yoo-ur goddam arsh. Lissin up, home-ee, I hee-ur thursh gonna bee sum fine bitch akshin go-eeng down in the Tarburt 'hood thuh night. Wurd!

Maybe it's appropriate. Like Native Africans and Native North Americans and Aboriginal Australasians, we Gaidheals were stripped of the rights to our own land, our own heritage. In our case – most humiliatingly – we were rounded up like sheep to make way *for* sheep. Treated like the scum that scum wipe off their boots so that other scum can look down on them. Our language, code of dress, social structure, customs and land all stolen from us. (Legally, according to laws that had nothing to do with the laws we already lived by.)

Nowadays, colonized by a nation of shopkeepers, we're a nation of shopkeepers' assistants.

Gaidheals especially are discriminated against to this very day. And am I right – invisible bigotry is the worst kind of all? Damn fucking right an I'm right.

Christ and the Holy Ghost on a tandem – there's kids growing up today who haven't even heard of the Highland Clearances. My blood boils.

---

* Tshoochter: phonetic spelling of teuchter, a derogatory term for a Highlander.

Sweat laminates my body.

I walk the rest of the way in a dwam, ideas shifting, finicky, melting like Dali-clockwork into wordless philosophies in my head. Vague and brilliant insights I will never clarify into words, and might paint but won't. I wonder if Eilidh will give me more of her period blood to paint with. After my blue period came my period period. But I was serious about that. I liked how the blood faded in time.

When I reach Karen Neònach's house I push through the heavy old door and shout, 'Burglars.'

Her voice bursts tinily from the back of the house. 'In the dying room.' Her name for the living room. She has more issues than the *Reader's Digest*.

The dust in the air catches my throat as I stroll through the hall. Karen doesn't dust her home – ever – because, 'My friend, we'll all be dust one day. Hell, it would be like brushing aside my future self.' Sometimes you have to suppose the relationship laziness has with creativity is akin to the one necessity has with invention.

Not smoking, sighing via a roll-your-own, Karen Neònach unsettles on the couch that's moulded her and jabs a remote TV on. The darkness pales into significance. 'News,' she remarks. 'Fuckit. Can't handle this.' She flicks the football on.

I hang by – I mean, I wait there, I'm not hanging myself – I hang by the door, feign interest. 'Who's winning?'

'No one,' she drawls in her trademark chic sulk. 'One

team's losing slower than the other.' Her face almost brightens. 'Bloody goalie – so slow he barely makes it to the action replays.'

Ha ha, I say.

I stand, fidget. Football used to interest me, but only in so far as it was a game of two halves and nine vodkas. Why spoil a good drink with a stressful competition on an idiot box? I gave up on watching football when I realized that our national team had long ago given up on playing.

Thirsty.

Thirsty thirsty.

She looks at me, sees I'm edgy as a blind guy dancing on a cliff-top. She – I love this – throws the remote control at the TV. *Clang*.

She unrolls to her feet. 'C'mon to the kitchen. Refreshments.'

We take facing seats at her battered old kitchen table with a bottle of Jack Daniel's and two glasses already set out. The table's an antique a bunch of us ruined one night drunk out of our skulls playing games with out-spread fingers and a knife. Karen's parents – doctors, from whom she inherited this house – had died in a car crash in France just a fortnight previously. None of us has ever managed to get Karen to really talk about it; common sense – which isn't common – none the less dictates that she must be bottling up more than all the distilleries in Scotland.

I still have a couple of scars, but the table came off worse.

Anyway, I'm half an hour late and impressed that she hasn't opened the bottle yet. Her lipstick smile is freshly glued. The girls in Boots on Cromwell Street (fucking *Cromwell!*) decide what colour the weekend's kisses shall be. The coves are just grateful there are kisses, rose-red, easy-pink, drunken, bloody. A kiss is just a kiss.

I frown. 'What's wrong with proper whisky? Why the drink-it-for-the-shitey-image stuff? If you're gonna buy bog-standard whisky buy it peat-bog standard.'

'It's just the American alternative.'

'Fucking ass-kicking Americans, issit? I know who'd win in a fight or a fucking drinking contest. In the shitty brown corner, tastelessly dressed it's Jack "dark but handsome" Daniel, so called because when it's dark he's handsome. In the red corner, smooth operator, Johnnie "always goes the distance" Walker.'

Her lips wreathe themselves into a near-antagonistic smile. 'You gonna refuse it?'

'Hellandfuck no.'

She – perhaps because of my sarcasm – *half*-fills two tumblers.

'*Slàinte.*'*

'*Slàinte.*'

We clink glasses like people in spacesuits kissing.

---

* *Slàinte*: Gaelic. Cheers (literally, 'health').

Karen Neònach and I – guess what – have a kind of soap-opera will-we/won't-we tension about us that's been there since puberty, but which I usually think of as a should-we/course-we-fucking-shouldn't tension.

Her mouth has a curve that gives it a permanently satisfied look. I find smugness in any person other than me as appealing as a cold puke sandwich. If we lived in the kind of place where rich people lived, she would have married a moneyed arsehole by now and got some kind of work-free job in fashion or PR, the kind of job where she would organize parties and have expensive-wine-fuelled affairs rather than actually do anything. I doubt she'll be a good art teacher as she's the only person I know, goths included, who has never, not even when she was a child, been seen wearing a bright colour. Brown, beige, mustard and grey. She's like the moor at its dourest.

Still, one of many subdued reasons I really and truly love Karen Neònach, apart from having known her for yearsandyears, is that shortly after her parents died she phoned up a taxi at four thirty in the morning and begged the driver to take her fifty miles away to her parents' grave so she could tell her folks just how much she missed them and bury her watch beside them. This one act skyrocketed her in my estimation.

'Tsup?' I ask.

'Mmm. Nothing much. Still thinking about it.'

(She means leaving the Island to go to teacher training

college, a sad detour for her, a kind of pauperish surren-
der. Typical for *Leòdhasaich*, to be forced into next-best,
or next-next-best.)

'And it's definitely art you want to teach?'

'Oh, yeah. Art looks like fun. Listen, who's your
favourite artist?'

I pause, swill a mouthful of American rockstars' piss.

'Apart from yourself, I mean,' Karen Neònach adds
sweetly.

'Van Gogh. But not for the paintings. For the ear.
That I truly fucking admire. That's worth twelve million
paintings.'

'You're full of shit.'

'Nope. I bet if anyone had that ear right now it would
sell for more than all his paintings combined. Am I
right . . . ? Damn fucking right an I'm right.'

She sighs. 'No wonder you became an artist. What
about other artists? Damien Hirst, Tracey Emin.'

'They're not artists. They're the stunted children of
advertising.'

'Others? Other influences?'

I raise my near-empty glass. 'This kind of stuff.'

'No, I mean – what's your take on life? Philosophy?
Have you read any philosophers?'

'Uh-huh.'

'Jesus Christ, never mind being a teacher, I think I'll be
a dentist. Or a Spanish Inquisitor. Who's your favourite
philosopher, then, Mr fucking talkative?'

'Thurber.'

She hesitates. 'Who?'

'James T-h-u-r-b-e-r. *The Seal in the Bedroom. Men, Women and Dogs.*'

'Eh? The guy we did in school? Night the bed fell and all that?'

'Him, yeah.'

'Why? He wasn't a philosopher, was he?'

I close my eyes in tight recollection. 'He wrote, "Alcohol, in attempting to resolve life's contradictions, produces vivid patterns of capital-T Truth which vanish like snow in the morning sun and cannot be recalled; the revelations of poetry are as wonderful as a comet in the skies, and as mysterious. Love, which was once believed to contain the capital-A Answer, we now know to be nothing more than an inherited behaviour pattern." And I'll drink to that. For that – ' I drain my glass ' – is genius.' I pour myself another one, impolitely large. Yankee gutrot. Why do I do it?

'So you don't believe in love? I can't imagine a life without the – the hope of love or marriage.' (I might be inventing this in recollection, but I think she actually shivers as she says this.)

A vivid-ish flashback cinemas my mind. Juanita and I spooned up in bed, her chest bobbing lightly in swift waves of sleep, me watching and listening to her breathing. From some part of her I could never reach she began muttering. Sleeptalking. At first the words were slurred, maybe Spanish but without the vowels. After this went on for a while she said in clear English that she would always love me and make sure I was always loved and we would look after each other for ever. My heart leaped and clutched at these words.

Soon, despite fighting it, my eyelids curtained down and I fell asleep. I had a sharp mini-dream, like a vision. Juanita was standing at the threshold of a low white Spanish house, smiling broadly, her bronzed arms wide open ready to receive me. I ran up to hug her. But when I got near her, her body froze and turned immediately into a grey statue. I hugged her cold effigy. A nebulous fear clouded over me and I turned round and walked away. But as soon as I had reached about ten feet away from the statue Juanita called me back. *Stornoway! Te amo, mi escosésito lindo!* I turned round and she was whole, she was flesh again. I grinned and ran up to her, but again she turned to stone as soon I got near. This happened again and again faster and faster until frustration or panic woke me up. I watched Juanita breathing deeply beside me in our tiny bedroom under the warm Spanish night. I tried to drive the dream out of my mind, but.

But we broke up soon after.

I look into Karen Neònach's brown eyes. 'Are you in love?'

'No, but—'

'No. Neither am I. No buts.'

'You're a cold-hearted bastard all of a sudden. Only

last week you were hugging everyone like you were seeing them for the last time. And all those girls – didn't you tell me you were in love with that girl in Edinburgh? And what about that obsessive one in Spain?'

'Haven't you heard the definition of endless love?'

'No.'

'Stevie Wonder and Ray Charles playing tennis together.'

'You think that's funny?'

'A wee bit, yeah.'

She shakes her head pitifully. I hate pity. This calls for a different approach. 'Okay, Karen, I'll be serious. I thought I was in love. Believing in love made life easier, but like all things it ran its course. Like believing in Santa Claus and dinosaurs and aliens and justice and – please, for the love of fuck, buy Scottish whisky, not this fucking cold tea mouthwash.'

'Van Gogh was in love.'

'Van Gogh was bonkers. Delirious. Heh! Yeah, that's why I like him. He was his own man. He had integrity. And the way like they say some kind of fish has Saint Peter's fingerprint on it, Van Gogh's brain had God's own fingerprint.'

'So at least you believe in integrity – that's something.'

'Yep. Integrity in fish, in animals, in birds and – much more rarely – in people.'

'Why?'

'If we all had integrity we'd all have meaning. We would have meaningful lives.'

'Uh?'

I stand up. 'I've got to go. Listen, Karen Neònach, I love you like the sister I never wanted, but you're poisoning me with this piss. You know I love alcohol like I love life itself, but this is enough to make me climb up onto the wagon and chain myself there.'

She glances at the bottle, which is, now that I really notice it, empty.

I pause, regain her gaze and hold it steadily. 'Anyway, what I mean is this, and if I die young or disappear up my own arse, or vanish off the face of the planet, or, worse still, become a Jehovah's Witness, at least remember this one shining truth: if you don't live for something, you'll die for nothing. I repeat for effect: if you don't live for something, you'll die for nothing.'

Fuckit, I forgot to hug her before I left.

Martin Monkeynut

Some fleeting years ago, Eilidh and I got stupendously drunk and I woke up with one of those ominous feelings: something is lurking just on the other side of my memory's perimeter, swift and irreversible as an electric shock. I know it, I can sense it coming closer.

I'm lying on my living-room floor, fully clothed, smelling too much like me and not enough like deodorant. My head is blitzkrieged. I get up and will myself towards the kitchen with a self-conscious clamber. Even a slow mouthful of *water* sends my head spinning out of control like a drunken rumour.

Surveying the rooms, I detect a powerful stench of puke.

I now remember Eilidh had thrown up a few times. I'd nursed her through that, stroking her hair like a kitten, cos I know how these things help, the soft details make all the difference.

(The more I think of it the more I hate people who say that people bring hangovers upon themselves. Trying to live here in Lewis as a teetotaller would drive anyone to the drink. And anyway, Lewis hypocrisy gives me the dry boaks.)

Co-dhiù, there was fuck all unusual in this – it was just a boring night at home in Lewis, no money to go to the pubs, so the evening dissolved in the companionable decanting of a domestic litre bottle of chicken and a few cans of Special. Simple.

But . . .

?

Think, man, think.

Right – I remember Eilidh had revived somewhat, maybe about two in the morning, after her third-time-lucky puke and we'd begun a giggly game of Vomit Euphemisms:

Chunder.
Pray to the porcelain god.
Chuck up.
Reverse feed.
Do a technicolour yawn.
Barf.
Call Huey.
Release the multicoloured hostages.
Make an Irish pizza.
Gabble on the great white telephone.
Drive the porcelain bus.
Launch your lunch.
Revise the menu.

We had written them down in handwriting that looked more and more like the *sgròbings** in the dirt a hen from Garryvard might make. We'd had an argument over *Feed the seagulls*, which I reckoned only applies to ferry-pukes. The list was long and sloped off into an infinite illegibility.

We'd then stumbled into a discussion of the various places where we had succumbed to the mighty barf-monster. Fuck yeah, it became a Top Ten of – *Liquid Laughs*, that was another one. Eilidh's favourite place had been outside the Colosseum. Probably thousands of people were sick at the Colosseum back in its bloody heyday, when you think abo—

Oh oh.

Oh Lord, no.

Now it's coming back, the memory, the thing that should not be, like a tide of puke itself . . . Ah, fuck . . .

!

Eilidh always gets excited about foreign countries – actually, about any fucking place that isn't Lewis. Hadn't she switched the computer on, got out the credit card and . . .

I look over to the chair in which Eilidh had last been slumped. Two pieces of paper with what looks like – but Christ, surely can't be – *Dep* and *Arr* times noted down in as-neatly-as-I-can-in-this-condition scribbles on unpeeled whisky label. Glasgow – Fiumicino.

* *Sgròbings*: Stornowegianized Gaelic. Scratchings.

Fiumicino, is that in . . . ?

*   *   *

Six days into our dubiously funded trip to Rome, we are practically Italian. That's almost an advantage of being a fucktup *Leòdhasach*. Insecurity loves disguises, loves adopting new roles. You can't figure who you really are, so you can be anyone. I always get a thrill out of being in a different country for the first few days and seeing, say, a red Fiat Uno and I'm about to wave to Seumas Shithead when I remember it isn't his car, it can't be. I'm in a new place. *And* I *feel* new. Being new is good. (Memo to self: get Kathy Crayons to design a chameleon tattoo around that mottoette, and find out if there's such a thing as white tattoo ink.)

My superfuckingdefining *Leòdhasach* Abroad experience occurs that sixth night in Rome. We're sipping explosive thimblefuls of whisky in a bar, a short amble down the Via Volturno. We've seen none of the touristy sights of Rome yet, apart from the Colosseum flukily glimpsed from the end of a street. The grand amphitheatre looked so laughably un-colossal I decided visiting it at all would be a disaster, a failure of enchantment, like a magic trick explained. I felt we were surrounded by beauty enough – in the people as much as the architecture. A multitude of pulchritude.

Every second person is Audrey Hepburn. We love to gulp in the elegance of the Romans, their easy perfections. A darker sightseeing, hidden by cheap airport shades. One day Eilidh wakes up with a scribbled-on beermat in her pocket. The handwriting is mine:

> *sunhappy café*
> *absorbed in Glamour magazine*
> *picking her nose*

As for excursions . . . we've seen a lot of bars. We haven't taken a single photograph; we have no idea what Rome looks like before midday. The late afternoons are hot enough when we awaken to the sun's cancerous throb. I like the way my sunglasses bruise the light. I wear them indoors too, an act that could result in someone trying to kick my head in back home in Lewis.

The bar is raucous; immaculate Italians – some, surely, no older than thirteen – are barking mellifluously and gesticulating like those guys on airport runways. Clouding the table at which Eilidh and I sit, a comfortable whisky-and-on-holiday relishing silence.

Suddenly my eyes snap and my neck whips in the direction of the bar. Is that . . . ? I feel a stunning change of consciousness coming on.

It fucking can't be.

Martin Monkeynut.

Martin Monkeynut, as I live and fuck and breathe.

Pigs right now are flying in formation over Springfield Road.

It looks like him: leaning at the far end of the bar, he's too far away for me to catch the language, never mind the cadence of his accent. I scowl. What in the blind motherfucking blazes would *he* be doing here? In Rome, furchrissakes? Martin Monkeynut, the semi-literate, concrete-boned giant, with knuckles like doorknobs, hair blacker than a blind man's depression, who I'd chased footballs with, rocketed on swings with, tremblingly cliff-dived with, and hurled, enemywards, toilet-concocted stinkbombs with throughout those eternally lessening early Stornoway summers.

Martin Monkeynut, my once-upon-a-time sparring partner, my bloodbrother for ever, my quick-to-temper quick-to-amnesia comrade, my Hutch, my Tonto, my Chewbacca, my buttergloved goalie, Martin Monkeynut, the clumsy gorilla who believed I was allowed to stay up until midnight any time I wanted, who believed I had once been out fishing and had seen a shark bigger than ten buses in a line, who believed that there were still dinosaurs in China, who believed that if he swallowed one more piece of chewing gum – cos six is the maximum – then his stomach would stickily clog up and stop him from swallowing ever again.

Martin Monkeynut, the big, gawky, gullible brute, my faithful, thickwitted sidekick – and now he looks suave –

yes, truly fucking *suave* – smiling with friends, in his posh, muscular suit, here in the sunhappy heart of Italy.

> *Martin Monkeynut, raw as a peat*
> *If only his brain was as big as his feet.*

Nobody, I bet, calls him Martin Monkeynut now. Only very rarely does he even recall that nickname, and it triggers scenes as if from a godawful, near-forgotten B-movie. His coolness – it seems to me now, a natural, jazzy, inimitable, total fucking Sinatra coolness, all slick suits, sharp cheekbones and warmly distant eyes – must have begun to emerge after my inhibiting control had ebbed and vanished more completely than fucking innocence. The thought strikes me like a lightning flash from hell: Am I *jealous* of Martin Monkeynut?

> *Martin Monkeynut looks like a* ceàrd*
> Sounds like a frog and smells like a fart.*

Martin Monkeynut – who had always worn those too-small, grassy-kneed dungarees, and hadn't been scared to use bad words in the playground because no one would tell on the biggest boy in the class. Yeah, everyone teased him with playground songs, but *only ever* behind his back.

---

* *Ceàrd*: Gaelic. Originally, a smith or similar workman, nowadays used pejoratively – 'tinker'.

Martin Monkeynut – my minder, as reliable as he was gullible . . . what potential did he have, in those days, to access a world of cappuccinos and Vespas, of easy chic and sophisticated passions? In those days, what he knew best was how to be raw and compliant, a willing guinea pig.

> *Martin Monkeynut he's so full of shit*
> *Whenever he talks he smells of it.*

His father, a gardener, had tired of the relentless Lewis weather and moved the family – where? to London? – just before the Niccy.

> *Martin Monkeynut's wrong in the head*
> *Cos his parents are cousins and he's inbred.*

I lost touch, of course, in no time at all and the little part of my mind that would, from time to time, think about him had somehow decided that he was a clunky surgeon (Eilidh-speak for mechanic) and, furthermore, that he was one of those people whose lives stop quietly like a clock in a long-abandoned house.

Yeah, these people go on living their lives, unfulfillingly filled with for-money-not-cos-I-want-to jobs, cliché-soaked pubs, averagely average marriages, unmarvellous children, yappity dogs, tidy-ish houses, ample lawnmowers, sporadic debts, footballing bigotries, occasional holidays, vicarious soap-opera excitements, random diseases – the whole depressing shebang.

But fuckit, their real lives are frozen in School Time. The day they set off the fire alarm, or swore at a teacher, or indulged in a legendarily reckless piece of vandalism, or scored a league-winning goal, or cycled off the pier for a bet, or pissed on the headmaster's car like a dog, or set off fireworks in a graveyard, or shoved an envelope full of dogshit through the minister's letterbox, or broke an arm climbing a tree with hands greasy after Cheeky Chips; these are their high and remembered moments.

Total and spurious fulfilment.

And thenceforth these people are dead in the shadows, because your own life must move on, chasing its elusive spotlight.

I mean *fuck* – who would have believed that we can make a leap scot-free into, as it were, the remembered landscapes of a foreign country, in which we can start again, with an entirely wished-for disguise? (In Lewis you're brought up so fucking conservatively most kids believe that socks, like shoes, have a correct left and right.)

And there Martin is, laughing among the in-crowd, the crescent moon of his beautiful, stylish friends, in a shiny bar in glorious Rome. I rise to my feet, scraping the chair away from me.

Eilidh looks up abruptly. 'Going to the bar?'

'No. Well, yes. I've just seen someone I think I might know!'

She half smiles, half frowns. 'Fuck off – you *serious*?'

My eyes fixed on Martin, I nod. 'Yeah . . . unbefucking-lievable. I'm going over to see if he remembers me.'

I weave through the tightlycrowded bar, jostling here and there – *Scusa!* . . . *Permesso!* – yielding to this fucker's push, that fucker's swagger, twisting and turning, being turned being twisted, saying '*Scusa!*', hearing '*Scusa!*', winding my slowmotion way over through the smoke towards their gorgeous harmonious laughchattering semicircle, towards Martin, who is throwing his head back with merriment, now and then hidden by dark Italian heads and raised *Cin-cin!* drinks, I plough on through the tall wide-shouldered men, I shimmer through the shapely perfections of women, some guy blows smoke in my fucking face and if I thought for one second he did it deliberately I couldn't care less cos there's Martin Monkeynut, furfuckssakes, Martin, whose expression changes more and more and fucking more the closer I get, some goddess of an Italian blone tipsily tips some of her white wine over my shirt and I don't even stop to hear the apology or chat her up I'm in too much of a hurry and so she has to do with the forgiving flash of a foreign smile, I just need to get closer to him and to shake his hand and show his new friends how fucking proud I am of him, a few more feet and I'll be there, Christ there were fewer people at the feeding of the five thousand, are they giving away free fuck-ing limoncello or something, I just want to shake this magician's hand and maybe a hug wouldn't be out of order in the exceptional fucking circumstances, and now I'm there, and here he is, Martin Monkeynut, glowing, confident, refined, admired, contented, urbane, smiling for Scotland, the Martin Monkeynut he should always have been, Martin Monkeynut who is not here in this swaying bar in Rome and who never was, who was never fucking here in the first place.

(. . . As I would find out three months after telling a friend this. For Martin Monkeynut had died in a grotty London bedsit, having overdosed on heroin, for God's sakes, aged twenty-two. Martin, I'm sorry; this episode's for you.)

A Password, Some Graffiti, a Man with a Name Like a Suitcase Full of Body Parts Falling Down the Stairs, and a Scary Bit

Drink has a lot to answer for, if only it could remember the questions. I have a fight with Eilidh in Italy. It brings our jaunt – well, my part in our jaunt – to an end.

I hope it hasn't brought an end to our friendship, which has lasted almost as long as I have. She reckoned I'm drinking too much. I denied it. The discussion esca-lated. I was too drunk, I suppose, to know what I was saying and the next day I simply couldn't remember what I'd said or for that matter what either of us had said or done. But Eilidh had lipstickslashed a note on my bathroom mirror saying she needed me right now the way I needed drink, i.e. it was a bad fucking idea, we had to have time apart for the good of our health.

I found leaving Italy relatively simple. We'd ended up somewhere north of Pisa – to this day I don't know how.

I took a perplexing train journey to Pisa in which I had to sit on a fold-out shelf in the narrow passageway, constantly up-and-downing to let toilet-users and new passengers past – with the nuns, as is customary in Italy, being the rudest.

I spent a night at a hotel in Pisa in a room with the most ornate bedroom ceiling I had ever seen but no nearby toilets. That ceiling was so amazing I never even noticed until I was checking out of the hotel that the room had no TV.

The Leaning Tower, like so many celebrities and things of that nature, was laughably small in real life.

An outwardly uneventful train journey to Rome had me deciding never to speak to Eilidh again, resolving to propose to her, demanding an explanation, apologizing, coldshouldering her and embracing her meltingly.

I'm haunted by something Karen Neònach said to me once. She said any kind of drunken behaviour was unforgivable because the drink only releases part of you that was already there. It's not the drink's fault.

Drink is a password, she said, not an intruder.

From that day on I began more fully to hate myself.

Rome is a few stifling degrees hotter than Pisa and I have to indulge in some extended and kind-of-gruff conversations with tourist information people to discover I'm flying from an airport called Ciampino. This involves a long subway journey surrounded by hairyarmpitted women and weary-eyed macho men, followed by a wait at Anagnina bus station, the ugliest place I've seen outside of either hell in my nightmares or Birmingham in sobriety. Dull grey pillars stand around the bus station like senile philosophers, proclaiming occasional brightly graffitied words:

Ti Amo

or

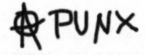

or

KARMA

These words slip under my emotional defences, panging with something like nostalgia. But I have no time to think of that. I climb aboard the late bus and find myself having to sprint to the check-in at Ciampino. Someone at a nearby desk is defeating bureacracy with precise and masterly bamboozlement: 'Still, I must insist you give me a one-way ticket to wherever you sent my bag . . .' I stop to listen for a moment, but a cursory glance at my wrist is like a starting gun.

I make it aboard the plane, just.

I'm desperate to sleep, to calm my scrambling heart-beat. Sprawled across the seat next to me, gangly-limbed as a spider, is a dark streak of misery who introduces himself as Reginald. He doesn't so much strike up a conversation as let it fizzle into being. One of those people who only opens his mouth when he has nothing to say.

'I'm in the City,' he declares pompously, as though I should be impressed. Well, why the bastarding fuck aren't you travelling business class? I think, and later wish I'd said.

Reginald talks about seatbelts with passion, a passion I don't exactly fucking share. When I call him Reggie he winces as though a particularly filthy rat has bitten his toe. 'Reginald. I prefer Reginald. I find it more – ah – becoming.'

More becoming? You're becoming a pain in the fucking arse. I sense one of my proudest moments brewing up.

'Reg-in-ald,' I say slowly, deliberately. 'Reg-in-ald. The word sounds to me like a suitcase full of body parts falling down the stairs.'

Result. His eyes flare.

Now he'll leave me alone, alone to nurse my mental breakages.

But no.

Reginald has made it his mission in life to bore people on public transport. His subject is seatbelts.

'I mean,' he drones, 'they're useless – quite useless – on planes. If the plane crashlands or falls into the sea a seatbelt isn't going to do much good, is it, what? Eh? No good at all. Might as well have an elastic band. What I want to know is – why do they have seatbelts in cars and planes but not in trains? You tell me that. Answer me that if you can. A seatbelt would help you at least as much in a train crash as in a car crash. The speed trains go at nowadays. But – no seatbelts. Not on trains. No. Planes have seatbelts which will do no one the blasted bit of good. But trains. Trains have nothing. Ought to have seatbelts, the lot of them. Every train in the country. That would make sense. But no. They put seatbelts on planes instead. None on trains. Not one. Unless the driver has one. That's an interesting point.'

Perhaps it does make sense but I'm tired and edgy. I'd gladly fucking strangle him with his seatbelt.

He continues. I try not listening. I play songs in my head. Rerun scenes from old films. Try figuring out which recent memories are dreams and which are real. Try doing the sixteen times table in Gaelic. Try imagining different ways of murdering someone with a seatbelt. No good.

I clear my throat, clear it well. Something's about to happen. I think for a moment or three while he monandonandonologues. Then –

'Excuse me, Reg,' I interrupt, 'but I have a lot on my mind right now and my life is in such a mess that your ditch-dull monologue on the seatbelt situation of selected modes of transport hardly constitutes a point of vague interest, never mind the fucking crisis you seem to think it is. To be honest, it bores me fucking stupid. Put on your seatbelt, don't put on your seatbelt – I couldn't care less if I tried.

'You see, I have problems of my own. Big problems, important ones. I can't hang around listening to your thesis on the merits and demerits of fucking seat fucking belts when I need to give serious thought to what is easily the most important decision I will ever make in my life.

'Can't you see how enormously unthrilling it is to be sitting – to be *trapped* – next to the most boring man on the planet? Of course you can't, because that man is you, Reggie, *you* are the most boring man on the planet, and you can't sit beside yourself, though God knows I wish you could.

'And you can wipe that Mr-Outraged-of-the-City-of-London look off your face because at least I've given you something to think about other than seatbelts, a little spark of interest, a story to tell your friends, if you have any, which I doubt, because you, Mr Reginald Bletherington Arsewipe or whatever, are the most tedious person I have ever had the vapid misfortune to meet. You are actually convincing me that karma really exists, since, believe me, I am a bad, bad person.

'But *you*. Oh fuck, *you* – you score one hundred per cent, A plus with extra credit, on the boring test. You are the master of monotony, the lord of the long-winded; frankly, you are the supreme fucking prince of the pointless. Even *thinking* about how boring you are is giving me a dull fucking headache.

'I mean, are you retarded? Senile? Now, don't get alarmed, Reginald, because what I am doing is I'm telling you the truth. And honest to God, cross my heart and hope to die, strike me dead if I tell a lie, your banal, repetitive, tedious little speech is – sincerely. Sucking. My. Will. To. Live.

'I'm at a very low ebb right now, and violence is never an attractive idea on a plane. So for the benefit and safety of all the other passengers and to discourage me from taking my own life right here in front of you, would you kindly and permanently, for the good of humanity, shut. The fuck. Up.'

Reginald – naturally, I suppose – gapes at me for about half a minute. I stare him down. He snorts, then snatches the in-flight magazine from the seatpouch in front of him.

'That's right,' I say in as patronizing a tone as I can. 'You see if there's a nice little article for you in there about seatbelts.' I present him with something between a decorative smile and a pure shiteating grin. 'That'll be interesting for you.'

I close my eyes. Regret immediately wells up inside me. What kind of person am I becoming? From friendships to money to time, I'm losing everything I've ever had – including self-respect, which was only there in bargain-bin quantity in the first place. The urge rises in me to go to the toilet, sit down heavily with my head in my hands, and weep for ever. I groan – even that's useless, since it would mean Excuse-me-ing past spidery Reginald, and for the life of me I'm too proud and humiliated to do that.

Eventually, the humdrum lullaby of the plane's engines has me slunk into a vivid sleep. I dream I'm in an anonymous city. It's a grey afternoon. Ashen skyscrapers tower above me on all sides. The streets are deserted. Casual shop doors swing open on silent hinges like unspoken challenges.

Not a single person. All the shops and offices are empty. Walking along a cramped street, I think I see what might have been a dog (but seemed to me a giant rat) scurrying down a dark alley. When I take a closer look there's nothing there. I stop suddenly in front of a large office block. Wide mirrored-black doors. The sign above the doors is in a language I don't recognize. I feel impelled to enter the building, know obscurely that this is what's expected of me. The doors open in a smooth, drowsy manner that's both inviting and cautious.

My legs carry me robotically into the foyer, which is silvery-grey and minimally furnished. An ashtray and a newspaper (headlines illegible) lie together ornamentally on a low table. Behind the wide reception desk a computer hums. A screensaver flashes across its monitor – red words scrolling over a white background. I can't understand the language; there are three exclamation marks at the end of the sentence as if it's a suggestive joke or a smirking warning.

I become aware of a surreptitious movement to my left, and turn to see a lift come to land sighingly from above. The doors slowly begin to part. I thrust my panicking hands into my jeans, fumble around my pockets for – what? A weapon? *Anything*. And find nothing. The notion that I don't even have a wallet distantly irks me. The lift doors open further and further and –

the lift is empty.

My breath is coming in buckling, swiftmoving waves. My lungs clamour for oxygen. I try to turn; I need to dash out of the building, but my legs refuse to co-operate and instead propel me towards and into the lift. As the doors seal shut behind me claustrophobia enshrouds me. The lift begins to ascend. I look at the control panel, stare for a moment at the buttons. If the marks on the buttons are numbers designating floors, they're not like any numbers I've seen before: a twiggy calligraphy, like Arabic. A light leaps – at random, it seems – from one button to another. I stab each and every button repeatedly, but the lift keeps moving steadily upwards.

The walls of the lift are moving closer together. I'm finding it more difficult to breathe.

My chest heaves as though a great weight is crushing down on it. I kick at one of the walls, but when my foot lashes at where the wall is, it feels like kicking against thin air.

I punch the doors, but again it feels like there's nothing there.

I'm panic-stricken and nauseous and an uncertain realization grows in me that I'm in some kind of futuristic coffin, being drawn towards a menacing destiny, some dimly deserved penalty.

I try to scream and find myself mute – my mouth's as if glued shut. I flail hysterically, hurl noiseless, useless punches and kicks at the shrinking lift, which is now scarcely bigger than myself.

Abruptly, with a dizzy lurch, the lift smacks to a halt. The doors draw open and I fall gasping out into

open air,

sink to my knees, doubled up,

and pantingly get my breath back.

I seem to be on a bare concrete street.

After a moment I stand up and glance around. I'm not on a street at all, but on the flat roof of a tall building. The roofspace seems no bigger than a boxing ring. A cool strong wind pushes at me from all sides. There are no walls or railings around the edge of the roof. I resist the wayward temptation to go and look over the sides. I know the building is high: very few of the buildings round about reach as high. I want to scan the horizon, try to gauge from the city below where I am, but I suddenly remember the lift. I whirl round; the lift has vanished.

A gurgling sound from somewhere behind my shoulder sends me spinning back round. In a spot that a moment ago was empty, a grotesque thing sits playing. It's a fully developed human being (in fact, my horror on seeing it is tempered by a distant, but internal, sense of recognition). It's fully developed in all but its facial features. The creature, of medium-build, looks about five foot eleven. It sits there toying with an object, gurgling to itself. It has the appearance of an average young adult male in every aspect but the most terrifyingly obvious: its face is that of an infant.

The thing's movements are fluid, self-assured. The juxtaposition disturbs me – draining and unforgettable, like a death threat. Its body has the physique and demeanour of an adult, but its toddler face mews and chuckles continuously. I scrutinize it with revulsion and a growing fear. There is something all too contemptuously familiar about the creature from the neckline down. The posture and manner. The long black jeans. The dark, skinny-armed shirt. The proportion and details of the body, right down to its wiry thighs and moon-rimmed fingernails . . . this creature has my body.

Not a near-replica, superficially similar – it's a clone of me, accurate in every detail but.

But the face, the babyish face. The wide eyes, the dirty blond hair, the paintsplatterings of freckles, the serious toothless smile . . . the thing's face corresponds exactly with the earliest photograph I have of myself. The moment this thought claws my mind, the creature's tiny childish head looks at me as if registering my presence for the first time.

Acknowledgement lurches in me. A sour pity – self-pity – churns acidly in my stomach.

For a few seconds we stare, eyes locked, regarding each other with an intense fusion of understanding and incomprehension, of familiarity and malevolence. Two long-separated parts of an antique mirror, one long buried in mud, the other submerged in a loch.

Uneasily, I break his shining gaze and look for the first time at the object in his hands. It's a clear cylindrical tube – a large syringe, with a razor blade in place of a needle. The syringe contains a liquid that changes colour mesmerizingly from golden yellow to crimson red to glistening black, then back to yellow . . . red . . . black . . . repeatingly.

I realize with a start that the colours have been almost hypnotizing me and that the creature is standing up. Wearing an expression between delirious, vacant stupidity and nascent cunning, he starts walking towards me. His slackjawed burbling laughter drops intermittently to a dirty titter, punctuated all the while with white slavers of drool, curved like transparent little sickles at each corner of his infant mouth. As he approaches he waves the syringe at me like a trained knifesman, but gibbers and gestures like a school bully, a monkey.

With each step he takes towards me I take a quivery

step back, sweating, conscious that the edge of the roof
– i.e., the end of my life – is near.

And coming nearer.

The wind gushes around me like a river in spate.
Taunting.

I halt, take a rapid glance over my shoulder, certain
that the edge is only two or three paces away. My heart
makes a fist of itself. I'm on the edge.

I tighten my calf muscles and lean forward slightly to
hold my balance. The creature almost leaps with joy.
His guttural twittering increases to a pitch of insane
merriment.

'Please – *don't*!' I want to shriek – but can't. I want to
ask him if he realizes who I am, that we are—

With a venomous squeal of exuberance, the creature
draws his arm back and readies to ram the bladed syringe
heartily into me. As he does so, my body jerks away from
the glinting razor's point and before I know it I'm tilting
back – too far back – over the edge of the building – the
building is already pulling up and away from me. As I
plunge earthwards, the wind prods and buffets me. My
face contorts into an unvoiceable scream.

The building flies upwards. The creature grins and
gurgles and waves as he rushes away from me. With a
greater and greater urgency I make swimming motions,
struggling to rise again, but I'm falling more and more
and more quickly and I know I'm about to hit the grou—

'Ow!' I let out a shriek as a massive electric needle explodes in my heart, sending it leaping against the wall of my chest in a fizzing surge of adrenalin.

My body jerks upright, stupefied, into a sitting-up position. I hear a dozen mouths trying to stifle embarrassed laughter. Sweat swims down my forehead. Powerfully blinking, I look around.

I'm on a plane. People around me are giving me bulletsharp but all-absorbing glances and trying to contain indelicate laughter behind hands, behind blushes. I run a shaky hand through my hair, which is dripping with sweat.

I remember. I'm flying home from Italy. Italy of the drink and the decadence and the disagreements.

The last few hours come brokenly to mind. Becoming aware of a presence other than the settling sniggers of the other passengers, I turn to find somebody sitting beside me.

Ah, fuck. The Reginald guy. He looks me full in the eye, gives a snort of derision, then sticks his nose contentedly into a magazine.

I shake my head, rub my eyes.

Public masks. And private.

A real man would apologize to Reginald.

Not me.

Not me.

The Sound of Nothing Happening, Followed by Some Things Happening

I wonder if it's time to go back into the world again, the straight-edged world where people neither agonize nor slowly poison themselves. I begin by putting the phone back on the hook, first time in weeks.

Nothing happens.

Sometimes I like the sound of nothing happening, especially if there's an invisible tension involved, like gazing out the window when snow is imminent, or like watching someone in a silent room when they're thinking hard – maybe they're sitting an exam, or being CCTV-monitored in a police cell, trying to get the story right. I *love* the almost visible sound of people thinking.

But the sound of nothing happening is treasonous; it can also be hurtful. Today the sound of nothing happening is the sound of loneliness and doubt and self-disgust; it's the sound of a Lewisman being a Lewisman on his own with nothing to do but be himself.

I switch the radio on – and regret it. Those braying

upper-class English accents are forks in my ears. I put a CD on instead.

Counting Crows. 'Perfect Blue Buildings'. It is sad and mysterious like someone lonely in a hospital or like a beautiful woman waiting in a train station in mourning clothes and fire-engine-red lipstick.

I get to remembering a time I saw Counting Crows in concert, during the days when songs like 'Raining in Baltimore' would make me weep. Remembering it makes me feel human, not in the familiar flawed way, but in the less familiar flawed-but-happy way I once used to glimpse.

Man, I don't want to do this, but I long to intensify the effect of the music, so I go to the kitchen for some wine – a box, I mean – and cut into it with apprehension.

A few (pint) glasses later, I'm listening to 'A Long December', a song that none the less never goes out of season since it's simultaneously depressing and uplifting, the way the best songs are.

I've got the old blue guitar out and I'm looking at it. It's funny to think that once-upon-a-not-so-very-long-ago life was as sexy as a new guitar shining in the high noon of a balmy spotlight, to think that future was not a word to be scared of.

Ah, well. I had some great times busking.

Here I am, sipping wine with the Counting Crows and looking at my guitar. Life is cordial enough, sometimes. *Stornoway*, I'm thinking to myself, *You're a legend*.

Or: *Hey, you're Stornoway the Legendary Artist. The Artist Who Made a Difference.*

I worry for the quintillionth time that I haven't yet designed a snappy autograph.

Am I somebody yet?

Is local infamy more punk than international fame?

Or do I secretly crave the day my art will give me income tax problems?

Am I not still pure (– in my art, I mean)?

What about the Airfix model planes I'm going to decorate with peace symbols, box up and post airmail to world leaders?

The CD I'm going to make that's entirely composed of looped recordings of the Dalai Lama giggling?

The T-shirt I'm going to design as a homage to Magritte – '*Ceci n'est pas une bagpipe*'?

The enormous glass, canvas, lipstick and bone sculpture I'm going to make out of this:

boy meets girl boy meet
meets girl boy m
meets girl boy me
meets girl boy me
meets girl boy me
meets girl boy me
meets girl boy m

boy meets girl boy meets girl boy meets girl boy meets
boy meets girl boy meets girl boy meets girl boy meets
boy meets girl boy meets girl boy meets girl boy meets
boy meets girl boy meets girl boy meets girl boy meets
boy meets girl boy meets girl boy meets girl boy meets
boy meets girl boy meets girl boy meets girl boy meets
boy meets girl boy meets girl boy meets girl boy meets
boy meets girl boy meets girl boy meets girl boy meets
boy meets girl boy meets girl boy meets girl boy meets
boy meets girl boy meets girl boy meets girl boy meets
boy meets girl boy meets girl boy meets girl boy meets
boy meets girl boy meets girl boy meets girl boy meets
boy meets girl boy meets girl boy meets girl boy meets
boy meets girl boy meets girl boy meets girl boy meets
boy meets girl boy meets girl boy meets girl boy meets
boy meets girl boy meets girl boy meets girl boy meets
boy meets girl boy meets girl boy meets girl boy meets
boy meets girl boy meets girl boy meets girl boy meets
boy meets girl boy meets girl boy meets girl boy meets
boy meets girl boy meets girl boy meets girl boy meets
boy meets girl boy meets girl boy meets girl boy meets
boy meets girl boy meets girl boy meets girl boy meets
boy meets girl boy meets girl boy meets girl boy meets
boy meets girl boy meets girl boy meets girl boy meets

after the apparently true story that, when William Faulk-
ner was kicked out of his Hollywood scriptwriting job
for being an alky, they found only two things in his desk:

an empty bottle of whisky (okay, it was probably
whiskey, but allow me this one contrivance)

and a piece of paper on which he had written 'boy
meets girl' five hundred times.

Why are Scottish literary anecdotes so pathetic in
comparison? Ah ha ha ha, wait till you hear this one –
Tavish MacTavish said, when asked about the messages
in his poems, 'If you want messages, go to the supermarket.'

Are all the really juicy stories being hidden from us? Is
there a secret vault somewhere in which some crusty old
academic is collecting and archiving all the sick, funny
and grisly stories detailing Scottish authors' decadence,
dissolution and debasement?

I hope so.

Maybe I'll get [DELETED] to spill some yarns. I could
certainly cause a literary brouhafuckingha if I made a
great art project out of all the Scottish literary scandals.
Wouldn't even need to make any of them up. But
[DELETED] won't speak, I know that much.

Fuck, my art is growing desperate. Restless.

Should I leave Lewis again?

Norway, for the fishing? Nah, drink's too expensive.

Iceland, for the maidens? Nah, the best of them *were*
icy. And drink's too expensive.

Eastern Europe? Hungary – for Eva the Succuba, Eva-WhoIShouldn'tBeThinkingAbout, and for the mind-smacking history (and cheap drink)?

I'm tiring of Lewis again. Almost everyone's had or murdered everyone else, either actually or in fantasy. Everyone's influence on (or friendship with) everyone else soon becomes obsolete and pathetic and hateful; this is the inflated price of overfamiliarity. Everyone hates everyone else. The Maws* versus the Townies.† The Protestants versus the Catholics. The twenty new Presbyterian factions versus the twenty newer Presbyterian offshoots. All of which will soon have a congregation of one, ministers included. The *Leòdhasachs* versus the *Hearachs*.‡ Everyone with an above-room-temperature IQ versus the bongilees.

Aye, familiarity breeds contempt. But 'paradise' comes from a Persian word meaning 'walled garden'. In other words, a kind of island.

Nothing makes sense, which is why I am trying not to think these days.

I love red wine. Like putting fresh blood into your blood. The warm flush, very much like a harder drug.

I drink some more.

---

* Maws: Stornowegian. Unpleasant and patronizing term for people from the countryside, somewhat similar to 'bumpkins'.
† Townies: Stornowegians, obviously.
‡ *Hearachs*: Stornowegianized Gaelic. People from Harris, i.e., southern neighbours of the *Leòdhasachs*.

One day they'll ban wine.

Eventually, of course: Drrriiinnng. Drrriiinnng.

The phone is on the table beside me. I suppose that since I've reconnected it I might as well answer.

I'm not going to slur. 'Normal service has been resumed. Hello?'

'Fuck's sakes. Hallelujah. He is risen again. Where the fuck've you been? No, don't tell me. I know where you've been. Why the fuck have you been avoiding me?'

'Eilidh, *a ghràidh*. I swear I haven't been avoiding *you*. I've been avoiding *everyone*. I needed to spend some time doing not much.'

'But you don't do anything anyway. I've been worried sick.'

'Sorry.'

'Jeez, I went round loads of times. I was starting to get really worried this time.'

'Ach, I was like an astronomer – I needed space. Not space from you. From stuff and from people.'

'What are you doing now?'

'Just sitting here at home.'

'You're sitting on that fleabitten old armchair listening to the fucking Counting Crows – I can hear them as loud as I can hear you. And I can tell you've been drinking. And I bet you're staring at that fucking guitar.'

She got me. See what I mean about people here knowing you better than you know yourself? 'Uh-huh.'

'Why the fuck do you always stare at that guitar? It drives me mental. I'd see the point if you played the fucking thing, but sitting staring at it . . .'

It's a good question. Deserves a good answer. 'Well, you know. Other than my contact lenses, it's the thing that's been with me the most, travelled everywhere with me. It *knows* me.'

'Godforfuckingbid that you would place a human being higher in your affections than a wooden fucking guitar. I don't know why I bother with you . . . Are you coming round?'

'Sorry, Pink Panther. Too comfortable in my wine and song. Small steps.'

'All right. Drink. Drink yourself stupid. I heard about you making a fuckwit of yourself in the pub the other night. The sheer fucking disgrace of Golden Shower – *Golden Shower* – telling people you were an embarrassment. Aren't you totally fucking *humiliated*?'

'Eilidh, this is like a guilt thing and you know I don't do guilt. Don't pressure me. I make my mistakes and I forget about them.'

'Fuck you then,' she snarls sweetly.

'Language,' I caution.

'Ah well, you just keep on drinking. Drink yourself sick. D'y'ever remember that time I had to take you to the hospital when your heart was racing and you thought you were having a fucking heart attack?'

'. . .'

'Well, the way you're heading, one day it *will* be a fucking heart attack.'

'Eilidh, I was kind of *happy* sitting here.'

'Sitting there drinking yourself stupid. You're going to end up a down-and-out, you know.'

I sigh. Fuckssakes. Well, if it's misery she wants – 'I'll end up in a hole in the ground, and so will you and so will everyone.'

'All right, keep drinking. Ignore your friends.'

'Look, I've needed to be on my own recently and I still do, for just a little longer. I thought it was peace, clearly it was neglect. If I've made a mistake then as the man in the orthopaedic shoes says, "I stand corrected."'

'Fucking drown yourself in drink and see if I care.'

She puts the phone down. Slammed, I suppose.

I put on a Ramones CD – *Halfway to Sanity* – and sit there drinking my red wine and looking at my blue guitar, which I once used to play on rich bustling streets in cities all over the world. Streets that were energy and potential solidified.

Next track. More wine.

Next track. More wine.

New CD. The Wedding Present. *Bizarro*, for the immensity of 'Kennedy' and the raucous heartonsleeveness of 'Brassneck'. Some bands have guitars so big and lyrics so open-wounded that you don't know whether your eyes are bleeding or your ears are crying.

New box of wine. Musta spilt some of the last one.

Sooner or later, inevitably: Drrriiinnng. Drrriiinnng.

Eilidh again. She screams various things at me – obscenities, advice, criticism, I don't know. All of the above and then some, I s'pose. You don't need the specifics in any conversation where you've to hold the phone a couple of feet away from your ear.

After a few minutes I move the phone close again and say as soothingly as I can, 'Eilidh, don't be unhappy. There's enough of that shit in the world.'

'FUCK YOU! I'm going out on the town. You can stay at home like the world's biggest sad-act. You think I've nothing better to do than sit at home worrying about you? I'm off out to The Heb for a dance.'

'Well, good,' I say sincerely. 'I hope it's fun.'

'FUCK YOU! And I'm going to sleep with the first arsehole I meet.'

'Eilidh, did we get married during one of my blackouts?'

'FUCK YOU!'

'Are you jealous of me spending time with my guitar?'

'FUCK YOU!'

'You think that if I drink by myself you have to get drunk with the first fucking knuckledragger you see?'

'FUCK YOU! I'm off out cos *I've* got a fucking life.'

'I know you love me—'

And I wanted to say something about my fucking life. But she's already hung up. Shame. Shame shame shame. I never saw her again.

An Interruption by Kevin MacNeil

I received a phone call from a Tarbert number, the voice incoherent but for its desperation. It was R. S., pleading an emergency of some sort – loss my fckn wallet, dno where th fuck I am, think my breathing sn't working right, can you come and clect me. Sa lass time, fuck mnever drinking again san accident, slipt off the wagon.

'You were never on it, pal,' I murmured, muggy-headed. I rolled over in bed. It was 3.30 a.m. 'I've no car remember?'

But he'd already put the phone down. Or worse. R. S. had often teetered between eccentricity and out-and-out derangement.

Stornoway is an amazing town. There are a great many places in the world where you cannot phone up a friend ring ring ring in the middle of his dreamy rejuvenation and ask him to drive you forty or so miles to pick up a drunk. My mate Murdo's a true friend, though, and he drove me there with careful speed, unquestioningly. He'd have lent me the car too had he not needed it for work in the morning (which also meant he had to drive all the way back after he dropped me off). *Tapadh leat a-rithist, a charaid.*

Tarbert was eerie and self-conscious at that time in the morning. The yellow buzz of the streetlights was like a kind of ceaseless nagging. I was worried. I couldn't find R. S. anywhere. I checked and kept rechecking the phone boxes, but it was as though he'd vanished. Tarbert is a small town, little more than a village. We hadn't passed any cars on the way down, so he couldn't have hitched a miraculous lift.

The water in the harbour glittered with a malevolent beauty around the ferry. And it was to the water, not the phone boxes, I most frequently returned.

*   *   *

As the sun began the uniquely *Hearach* version of its ascent, I gave in and decided to walk a little bit out of Tarbert to clear my head, growing groggier by the minute.

The fresh wind revived me somewhat, but I fell into a daydream about the possibilities of R. S.'s life before I knew him. Much of his life remained a mystery. Often, on hearing an obscure town mentioned on the news he would describe exactly what kind of place it is, how friendly or hostile the locals are to street musicians, how good the coffee is, how strong the drink.

As I walked along, stiff and weary like an old man, I

heard a mild groan, more like a soft whimper, and almost simultaneously caught a red glimpse of lazy movement in a ditch a few yards up the road. My legs forgot their tiredness, sprinted me there in seconds.

And there he was. Scotland's new writing talent, scrunched into himself in a ditch, smiling and murmuring, mudsplattered and dribbling over his new red sweatshirt.

Thank God he was okay.

I let him sleep, sleeptalk, sleepfidget for an hour or two.

I sat in the ditch with him, half listening to his burbling, mostly wishing I'd brought a book to read. When Tarbert began to wake up to the sound of the ferry traffic and the near-human screeching of seagulls as they wheelingly prodded and needled the sky, I roused Stornoway from his comfy trench.

'Rise and shine, superman. It's a brand new day.'

His confused look confused me; he wasn't surprised, it seemed, at waking up in a ditch, but he had to blink rapidly to assimilate *my* presence there.

I sighed. I knew he had no recollection of phoning me. 'You phoned me last night.'

'Oh. What's up?' he asked, casually.

I hesitated. Grinned. 'Ach, nothing much. Let's go down to the toilets and get you cleaned up. Then breakfast in a café, then get the bus home to Stornoway.'

He scratched his head and yawned indulgently as a cat. 'We're not in Stornoway?'

*   *   *

The bus trundled on through the cold Hebridean day. The air was bright outside and the mighty Clisham gleamed rockily, parried with the occasional cloud, wow-ing the American-voiced cameras at the front of the bus.

At Balallan a young mother climbed aboard, carrying a little child. She slipped into the seat in front of us, and the child, being hugged and backpatted, looked at us over her mother's shoulder and cooed and gurgled and stared at us with gigantic swimming-pool eyes. A clown's grin spread across my face. I waved cartoonishly at the wee girl.

R. S. landed a sharp punch on my arm. 'Quit it, Stanley Laurel,' he muttered. His tone was hostile.

I glared at him, speechless.

'I'm moving,' he said, suddenly rising. He clambered over me and strode up the aisle to the back of the bus. I sat where I was, frozen in astonishment.

I looked back at R. S., now sunk in some inner sulk of his own at the rear of the bus. I turned back and gazed at the little girl, bouncily gurgurgurgling, a happy redness spread across her cheeks like wet ink. I waved again, wondering how much a child at that age understands. R. S. had once written a song indicating his belief that the most enigmatic thing in the known universe had nothing to do with relativity, with synchronicity, with symbiotic biology; it's a baby's first ever dream, that irretrievable, personal, colour-sealed, dawn-dismantled dreamscreen.

The wee girl smiled gummily, dribbled, chewed air.

I wondered when R. S. last felt a drop of that pure, mindless concentrate –

joy.

A familiar, overbearing shadow helicoptered, gloomering hungrily like a fat evil bee in the rear corners of my mind. It was anxiety, a portentous anxiety that arose every time I thought of R. S. and the destruction he was inflicting on himself. There was much I didn't know about him. I knew about his drinking, suspected that, like so many of my acquaintances, he was daft enough to be a dedicated smoker, too, of spliffs. His choice. His life. But.

Were there other drugs? What compelled him so doggedly to pursue his own self-destruction?

I once talked to him about how we all need human warmth. He'd nodded a beat then said, 'Yeah. Preferably blonde.' A rare, darksimmering cloud now settled in my mind. Anger at R. S.'s selfishness. I got up and staggered, shaken as the bus roundabouted into Stornoway. At the back of the bus I dumped myself heavily into the seat beside R. S.

'Is it the hangover? Why are you so callous today . . . ?' I started to say, but the words stuck in my throat. R. S. was staring out the window, eyes blank and red. Eyes moist, slowly dripping.

Instinctively, I put my arm round his shoulder, all the while pierced with the incongruous confirmation that R. S. was – *this* vulnerable?

'What's wrong, cove?'

Eventually he shook his head, as if to say, I can't tell you or, You wouldn't understand.

The bus arrowed shoogily into Stornoway Bus Station.

'You know by now that you can tell me anything,' I said. 'And if you can't talk about it – *write* about it.'

He sniffled, nodded almost threateningly. 'I will.'

K. M.

PART TWO

Everything's Bad for You and
Sleep Gives You Cancer

A Blue Guitar, a New Moon and the Inverse of an Island

Edinburgh. I was eighteen. Fed up of Lewis, ready to take on the world. I knew I had to leave Lewis when I got to the point where I was recognizing the sheep I counted when trying to fall asleep.

A blue guitar and a bunch of songs were my meal and my travel tickets. For a few months I squatted in a dun-coloured, brooding former factory in Craigmillar with a shifting shiftless mess of crusties, alcoholics and vacant-eyed drifters. We lived our own lives, kept out of each other's way, our social interaction amounting to no more than sarcastic comments about each other's looks and/or habits. Drunk or drugged, no one fought. No one could be bothered. It was an existence of tolerance and non-attachment. Suited me all right.

The capital city was the first stop in my world busking tour, partly because I didn't want to busk somewhere like Inverness, where *Leòdhasaich* went for shopping trips and were therefore liable to recognize me, and also because Edinburgh had an irresistible creative draw. It shimmered in my mind like a dim magical city swathed in nineteenth-century mists, populated with Jekylls, Hydes, artists, musicians, criminals: a city suffused in secrecy, whether under a sickly moon or a watery sun.

A few days into my Edinburgh experience the city is still unfamiliar enough to offer frequent fresh postcards of itself. Her streets are aged and gothic and I feel at home when a swirling autumnal fog descends over the areas I vaguely know. My mental map stretches from Princes Street's natural glamour and ridiculous shops, down through the pizza-strewn Bridges, past bustling, self-knowing George Square, through the schizophrenic Meadows and down calm, stately Dalkeith Road off towards Craigmillar and the squat, nestled squarely opposite a Hammer House graveyard.

The evenings are lit by a new, exhilarating silverwhite moon that looks and feels different from the familiar old Lewis moon, that inquisitive and contemptuous eye. The tired full moon I despised in my youth. The one that was God's torch blazing down over Lewis, scouring the raw moors and the curtainfidgeting streets for sinners.

This new eastern moon shines with a refreshing potential, casts a clear inviting light on the unexplored streets in my mind. My veins buzz with a dizzying abandon. An airy surge pumps my chest. I begin to half-believe in my potential. I can do what I want without gossip, without penalty, without that loathed nosiness masquerading as concern. I am an untethered boat.

For the first time in my life I am utterly anonymous. Far from the suffocating criticisms of Lewis.

That terrible ballast disappeared.

I take energetic strolls up Blackford Hill, marvel at the nighttime views of Edinburgh, a box of spilled jewels. There is a fantastic Twilight Zone-ish observatory on top of Blackford Hill and I sit on a bench nearby munching sandwiches and inventing absurd narratives about the science-fiction discoveries the whitecoated eccentrics are making inside. I'm a kind of alien myself.

I save busking money to go swimming in the Victorian quiet of the Infirmary Street Baths at eight thirty each morning. (The squat, of course, has no showers.) The swimming pool is, in my mind, the inverse of an island.

I quickly grow to recognize the unconcerned faces of the regulars and to appreciate the tacit acknowledgement that speaking is prohibited. We share a rippling calm, quiet-time in the early bustle of the city. Slow breast-stroking lengths in the cool chlorine hush.

Odd, to be swimming in that muted, near waveless rectangle of sea.

Odd, to be so enclosedly free.

These – these were my life's calm hours.

If I Don't Speak to Her Right Now I Could Quite Possibly Kill Myself

Saturday night, eight o'clock – and I have every intention of getting knocked senseless by drink; I'm looking forward to it hungrily. Shadowy motorbikes crouch at swaggering angles outside the pub. The wooden tables are animated by an energetic amalgam of bikers, goths, crusties, yahs, indie kids and even some normal people. As I amble nervously into the Pear Tree's moonlit beer garden, I absorb the hubbub of drinkinspired boasts, philosophies, jokes, worldchanging judgements – the usual pub bullshit. Booze wisdom. If only the drinkers ruled the world. I climb the steps up into the pub and order a pint of Special.

It isn't. I drink it at the bar. It's thickly watery and sweet-tasting. Not a great pint. 'Give me another with a large whisky.'

The barman recognizes me, serves me quick for the keep the change/have one yourself. Recognizes me for what I am, too, no doubt.

Suddenly my life begins anew.

This is how it happens.

Here She is.

If you want my advice – just try never to expect it.

Like the song goes, Aphrodite at a bar stool by my side.

I clear my throat. Never have I felt so imperfect, hunched clumsily as I am over two lonely drinks, with my lacklustre straw hair, my teeth like the Callanish Stones, my Concorde nose, my beady pissholes-in-the-snow eyes.

Her face shines with personality. A stranger, being so honestly herself, drinking on her own, smiling, is an act of trust. God bless the truth of a trusting person's inherent decency. Instinct, picking up on clues like these, tells me she has been well brought up. No pretensions. The delicious curve and blush of her cheekbones, a marble defence against the cold east coast wind. Her abundant, gleaming black hair shimmers like a mirage and is intricately French-pleated (she must be good with her hands). She sits there, slender and elegantly dressed in black velvet, her pink lips sipping red wine, the high-cheekboned star of my movie, her every motion exuding a swan-like grace. Her unblemished complexion seems to radiate a spiritual tranquillity.

Uh – perfection like this really exists?

I am sudden joy and apprehension. I feel as though my skin has come alive, inside and out, for the first ever time. The world tingles and sparkles, quickly forgets it was ever shoddy. The air between us is an organic entity. It's like up until this moment my living has been done for me – I simply breathed. Now I know the wonder of the insatiable and my mind is brimming over with warmth and a physical need to embrace this impossible human being.

I feel like my life has been leading me to this, my life has been a jigsaw puzzle, with a blank piece in the centre, her perfect predestined face.

If I don't speak to her right now I could quite possibly kill myself.

'Hi,' I grin. 'The least you can do is let me buy you a drink.'

She smiles back, shocked –

smiles!

'Why?' (Confused or/and intrigued.)

'Because,' I say with all the earnestness in the world, 'I'm in love with you.'

The Seduction Scene

Communication . . . Talk. (Drink. A little bullshit.) Chat. (Drink. A little less bullshit.) Tête-à-tête. (Drinks. No bullshit.) Whispers. (Drinks. Regret any bulls shat.) Secrets. (Drinks. Hurting to her beauty.) Whispers. (Drinks. Taking part in a miracle.) Secrets. (Drinks.) Secrets never to be told.*

* This scene is, you'll gather, somewhat abbreviated. Some reader participation is required, and I thank you for that. Your input was wise, imaginative and, indeed, wickedly seductive. (Oh all right, I'll tell you one chat-up line that never fails. You say, 'Excuse me, but you have a beep on your nose.' 'What?' (s)he will respond. You then reach over and gently squeeze her/his nose. 'BEEP!' Don't believe me? Try it.)

A New Way of Being Drunk

Hand in hand, we skip-dance along the street. She leads and I follow. I would follow her anywhere.

She talks of evening skylines and buildings that make you feel safe just by looking at them. She says that often at night when she walks the streets of Edinburgh she sees her home city of Budapest just around the corners and beyond the hills. She talks of it so vividly that – fuck – I can see it, although I've never been there. She fills me with an energetic urge to go there, to wander where she has wandered, to have been where she has been. I want to go there with her. I want that city to be a part of me like it is a part of her.

When I was about fourteen I felt a transient tranquillity that I re-experience each time I look into the seas of her eyes. I was out on the moorland near Tolsta, skiving off from school. In the distance, the mainland shivered in heat haze. I tilted leftways on the peat bank, shoogled a hip flask out of my back pocket. The flask silversparkled in the glutinous blueskied light, felt fleshwarm and disconcertingly smooth in my sweating fingers. I unscrewed the cap, tossed it away – a gesture that belonged more to Captain Moses than to me. The rum fumes, the paraffin bouquet, swam dizzily upwards, tinged with salt and potential, doing to my thoughts what the mist of belly-dancing heat was doing to my eyes.

I sat haltingly up on the open gash of the peat bank, as near to vertical as was sustainably comfortable.

Inhaling deeply, I raised the flask in a toast to the waves that were tirelessly quivering on the beach below. I nodded solemnly, whispered: 'To the sea that will take me the fuck away from this island the minute I turn eighteen.'

I swallowed a mouthful of the rum – which caught my breath, tight, like smoke – and immediately I gulped some more. The drink spread into my stomach, a sprightly lava. I settled back on my elbows. The moor pressed itself spongily against me. A few inches in front of my face, a wasp cruised past with its miniature chainsaw.

Out of the blue – the fainter blue, the bland, unknown sky – a broken shadow flitted overhead. I gazed up. A skylark was writhing in the near-cloudless sky, distant and happy, like early childhood, a stringless kite.

I glugged another mouthful of rum. My head lightened. Over the bay, a little cloud had appeared like spilled Tipp-Ex, a smudge of purity. Gradually it took on, for all the world, the droll shape and manner of an elongated man. I heard Moses' voice: 'Oh, yes. Legs that stop just short of the neck, scrawny body.' (Scratch-fizzle of a match being lit. Three puffs on the pipe and a three-beat pause.) 'He's a *MacLeod* all right – heh heh.'

I shuddered, swallowed more rum.

I sucked at the reluctant dregs in the flask, upended the flask for a moment, then threw it wholeheartedly away. It landed in the heather with a muffled indifference.

Groaning with skewed pleasure, I slumped back on the peat bank, shut my eyes. My blood was simpering with diesel.

I couldn't bear thinking about going back home, filled as it was with absences and the wrong tidiness.

The rum worked its magic and I felt absolutely at peace with my hollow self, with the ugly moorland, with the hungry sea. The more I looked at the sea the more it seemed to have the soporific rhythm of a high summer hammock. I fell asleep and dreamed I was a different person, a kind and thoughtful person whom people looked up to. I dreamed I was popular. When I woke up I was amazed to notice firstly that it was nighttime, meaning I'd slept for about nine hours and, more astonishing still, that I had actually cried in my sleep: tears of contentment.

That was a kind of happiness.

Is this new feeling of love a deeper version of that happiness? And if so, can it be final, or must happiness always be fleeting?

Eva brings out some good in me, good I never really knew I had.

I feel like I belong with her. The streetlights and the flashing torches of passing cars illuminate her face in all its depths of sweetness – snapshots of a potential life so impossible I couldn't even have dreamed it up. Her eyes are green planets slowly winking in the unworthy night. Her lips are like everfresh strawberries, dawnstained pillows, veils to an impossible passionstreaming cave. Her freckled nose is measured and angled to perfection. She has loosened her black hair, which now shimmers about her unblemished face like dark raw silk.

I'm not drunk any more, I'm stupendously in love, and Christ Almighty, what a fucking feeling, what an intoxication this is. I know, I feel certain . . . if only . . . if only I could have *this* instead I sincerely think I would never touch a drink again.

Destiny Says: When There Are Two People and One Bedroom – Fuck It, Let Love Blossom

Oh, Lord – please please please.

I've got to stay cool. 'This is a great place,' I say, trying to stay cool.

It's ten minutes later and I'm admiring her neat deep-blue and burnished-gold semi-minimalist flat on Nicolson Street. Her flat is on the second floor, above a chemist's with a sign in the window that gave us a breathless fit of the giggles: 'We dispense with accuracy.'

I'm falling more in love with her every passing moment.

The walls display timeless black-and-white photographs of a beautiful, river-divided city. Budapest.

'Did you decorate this place yourself?'

'Yeah, kind of.' She's perfect in every way. A Hungarian goddess, nineteen perfect years old. Eva.

I scan the flat. 'Just the one bedroom?'

'Yeah, no flatmates. I'm kind of spoiled like that.'

I've already told her about my squat. 'God, you're so lucky,' I say, shaking my head, wondrous with envy.

'Whisky all right?'

'Better than.'

I sink down into a lithe skyblue couch and take an acceptably overgenerous glass of Lagavulin.

Eva sits neatly down beside me, then sprawls back, snuggling her head into a cloudplump cushion.

(Life – really this good?)

I raise my glass. '*Slàinte!*'

'Cheers!' She takes a sip of her whisky, spills some of it on her silken blouse. 'Oops. Getting drunk.'

At the Pear Tree we'd had a lot to drink by her standards, a start by mine.

I'm in love. Fuck me. In love in love in love. Ridiculous thoughts are weaving in my head, and it isn't the drink. I take a mighty slug of the malt like it's weak beer. Wild thoughts. Futures. 'What are you going to do when you graduate?'

She pouts. Phenomenally. 'Who knows? This is my second last year. So after this it's back to Budapest for a year. And then . . . the usual arts graduate stuff. *Can I take your order here, please?*' The joke is a tired one, but coming from those immaculate lips, in her wordperfect English, it sets me laughing like a kid.

'What about you? Once you're a famous artist, what's left to do?'

'I'm going to write a book,' I say, surprising us both.

'A book? Really?'

'Yeah.'

'I don't believe you. I always wanted to meet a guy who could write a book.'

'Yeah, I'm going to write a book.' I say it seriously.

'That's amazing! What about?'

'Well, it's going to be my memoirs.'

'Well, here's something,' she says, sitting up. She puts her glass down on the floor, removes my glass from my hands, clinkingly lays it beside the other one, and leans in to me, 'to put in your memoirs.'

And her soft, hot, peat-flavoured lips set my lips on fire.

Sea-Sweat

Sea-sweat; in that tumbling, wavespuming, softcrashing togetherness, I turn to her with an invisible smile in my mouth and eyes.

'I can't believe it. I can't believe this.'

'Mmm,' Eva says and kisses me wetly on the cheek.

'Honestly, this is incredible. I never thought—'

'Hmm?'

'I never thought that – that you would be so – just so beautiful and that I would be – well – here, with you.'

Eva titters. 'And I never thought that I would be here with you, a rugged Highland artist—'

'I'm not!' I object.

' – here with you,' she says firmly. 'A rugged Highland warrior artist.' She giggles again.

'Are you taking the—'

'Ssshhhh!' she shwispers, like the waves. 'Ssshhh. Go back to sleep.'

As I slip under.

*

And I must have thrown my arm out into the sea's emptiness because I wake – or think I do – in the blanketing waves, water dripping all over my skin. For some moments my heart squalls, palpitates . . . then warmth and warm thoughts rise in and around me. Sweat. And the radiant heat of her naked body perspiring beside mine. Spurious emblem of a forgotten lighthouse, the bland thumb of candle we had failed to extinguish, threatens and gutters.

We drift in and out of a massage of sleep. Saltmouthed. Yielding to tides. Surfacing in each other's turnings, in dreams, either side of that littoral, wordless margin.

Her damp hair, glistening, furling like seaweed.

Her breath filling in, fanning out.

The lunar swell of her stomach, its hollow ebb.

Evidence. Those brinecrusted chambers.

Maybe the conversation occurs, maybe something very like it; maybe I dreamed it.

'Eva, were you – are you really drawn to me?'

'Mmmm. Really. Hey, like a line to a pencil.'

'I knew it.'

'How?'

'Because you told me.'

'Hm?'

'You told me in a conversation.'

'I did?'

'Yeah . . . the conversation I made up in my head, or dreamed, I think.'

'Hmmm. Ssshhh.' Her finger presses saltily to my lips.
The last nub of candle mutely coughs itself out.

How, in one fell swoon, our blue shadows plunged
that night into such a cool and resurfacing bitterness.

Fiction? Pardon?

Late afternoon in Edinburgh's Central Library and I'm trying to coax an English translation from gaunt, cobwebby Gaelic. I'm reconstructing the words of a Gaelic song from the great panegyric tradition, words that will suit a dark melody I've written on my guitar. The *bàrdachd** sang of the heroism of a warrior killed in battle; it sang his triumphs, his courage, his idealism. The warrior was eulogized as a great role model. As part of a wider art project, I'm rewriting the song as an admiring tribute to Kurt Cobain, the average young Gael's modern-day equivalent of a hero. I often come to this library when it's too wet outside to busk, too wet even for sympathy money.

Every so often an English voice flirts and giggles with a lazytongued American drawl at a nearby carrel. Shaking my head at the grave old font, I sigh and close the anaemic book; a thin swarm of dust bursts from the pages

---

* *Bàrdachd*: Gaelic. Here, specifically *traditional* Gaelic poetry / song.

like a cloud of midges. I stifle a dry cough and turn to Raymond Carver's *A New Path to the Waterfall*. I always balance library time evenly between working on songs or art projects and reading books that make me feel as if I'm alive.

I love Carver. In my fifth year of high school I wrote a dissertation for Higher English on Raymond Carver's work, inadequately detailing biographical information (the poverty, the alcoholism) alongside inept literary criticism (the rich and miserly use of language, the extraordinary intensification of the unelevated mundane). I worked hard, presumed I would get a decent mark even though I skived more classes than I attended. (I was simultaneously undergoing a formative and no less enlightening education out in the Castle Grounds.)

Mr Snow, our grey-faced, quietspoken teacher, handed everyone their papers back. Except mine. He stopped at my desk and paused for half a minute before speaking.

'You'll see me after class,' he said softly.

?

When the chairscrapings and the bagzippings and shovings had subsided, I was left alone in the class with Mr Snow's inscrutable gaze and a silence that left me increasingly and unfathomably guilty.

After some long minutes, Snowy, still staring at me, nodded almost imperceptibly. 'Mm-hmm.'

I swallowed.

Fidgeted.

Cleared my throat.

'I have not marked your paper.'

A troubled heat flushed over me, forehead to toes. I felt my face redden and trickle. Why in the hell not? What had I done?

And still he was looking at me in that maddening, emotionless manner.

'This is not to say I do not – ah – have some regard for what you did.'

A small wave of hope, and then a greater wave of confusion, washed over me.

I tugged at my collar. 'Yes, sir,' I said in a tone that was more question than statement.

('Sir' because Snowy was the only teacher I respected.)

'My boy,' he sighed, 'it is the convention within this department, if not this entire educational establishment, that when one is writing an assignment on an author of one's own choice, then that assignment is based upon a writer *who actually existed.*'

My jaw slowly spilled open.

'Oh, yes, boy. You can't pull the wool over my eyes. This is not to say that I did not admire the quality of creative thinking that went into composing an essay – or should I say a piece of *fiction* – of this kind. I do, however, question the wisdom of such a choice.'

My jaw hung open as I tried to cohere my thoughts. He actually believed that I had invented tersemouthed bluecollared poorasamaggot Raymond Carver. As I wondered what Carver himself would have made of this, a benign expression flickered over Snowy's face.

'Look, because what you did was, if nothing else, *original*, I am prepared to offer you, as it were, a deal, and a most agreeable one at that. I shall grade this exercise as a piece of creative writing and have it placed in your assessment folder accordingly. But you, my boy, shall go home tonight and complete the assignment,' his voice grew liltingly emphatic, *'on a genuine writer.'* He paused, glanced at the ceiling and then back at me. 'Living or dead, but *genuine*. Actual. Real. Legitimate. *Bona fide*. Authentic. Someone who was – or is – a person, and not the figment of a schoolboy's overactive imagination.'

To my inward horror, I found myself nodding obediently.

'The completed assignment shall be sitting on my desk at four o'clock tomorrow afternoon. Now, off with you.' He jabbed a finger at me. 'And don't be so smart in the future.'

Dazed, I gathered my schoolbag together and slouched out of the classroom, catching a last glance at Mr Snow as I pulled the door shut.

He was looking at my paper, shaking his head, chuckling wryly.

Isn't the Carver book in my hands real? And the panegyric song for Cobain? I flick through Carver's library-stenched pages, half smiling. I pause.

I haven't heard from Eva.

Not for a long time.

But her image drifts into my head unannounced at least once every waking hour and almost as often, I reckon, when I'm asleep.

I need to let her know just how special she is, how glowingly beautifully uniquely perfect. I want to hug her innermost self, to share her human warmth.

My eyes fall on the last poem in the book, a poem that's always panged in my heart like fruit suddenly ripening. 'Late Fragment'.

What a poem. Absolute recognition yearns in me like a wayward kitten.

The poem is a clear articulation of a hunger so deeply embedded within me that it seems to reanimate the me-est part of me, a part of me it has taken my whole life to discover.

A certain knowledge rises and asserts itself – without this love, without feeling myself *beloved on the earth*, I will remain incomplete.

I have never before surrendered to this admission.

Too tough. Too cool. (Translation: Too self-involved. Too drunk.)

Now, seeing this truth in black and white before me, I see why my sense of self has always felt flawed, why I'm an ongoing self-depleting disappointment.

I can only be me when I am with someone else.

*

I walk into the cold night air and head south through The Meadows. The yellow lights of the lampposts cast a cosy glow around the little groups of students standing or walking about laughing and gesturing animatedly. No matter how many times I walk through this part of the city, I never chance into Eva, nor – even more amazingly – do I glance more than once at any of the stridently beautiful students.

Cyclists and skateboarders whizz past, eccentric professors dash single-mindedly to libraries, classes, cars, pubs. As I watch them I grow aware of something. All of these people look happy. Naturally happy. Framed though they are by tired, sunken eyes.

I resolve to phone Eva. I want to let her know just how special she is, how perfect. I want to hug and reassure her, because this is why we're here: human warmth. Else why be?

I need to tell her how much, how gloriously much I love her, how she can feel herself – it will be the first time I've ever said the word out loud – *beloved* upon this earth.

Alexander Graham Bell, This Wasn't in the Plan

Drrriiing. Drrriiing.

Drrriiing. Drrriiing.

Etc.

Et fucking cetera.

C'mon!

One minute and twenty-eight seconds later: 'Hello?'

'. . . Eva! Hi!'

'Oh – hi there.' (Pause: her voice is not as phonogenic as it should be.) 'What's up?'

'Well, I-I've just been busking and sketching out songs and ideas, just been in the library an that, you know. I've – I've been missing you.'

'. . .'

This somehow isn't going to plan. My heart swoons. 'How have you been? I haven't seen you in ages. Everything going well with the course?'

'Oh, fine. You know.'

No, I don't. 'Right. Uh . . . well. It's been ages since

211

we met up. I was wondering if you wanted to meet up for a drink.'

A (forced?) sigh. 'I don't know – I'm so busy just now—'

She can't be talking like this. It doesn't make sense.

'Yeah,' I suddenly bark, 'and I'm busy too, but work hard, play hard, no?'

'. . .'

'Eva, is there something wrong?' – this with a small but sharp edge of panic in my voice.

Silence. Rasp-puff-fizzle of a cigarette being lit and breathed. A long inhalation. A smoky outsighing.

Desperation begins its quiet thrashing in my mind. I struggle to keep my voice steady. 'Eva, I'd really like to see you. I need to see you – to talk . . .'

'All right.' (Pause.) 'The Last Drop, then. Ten o'clock tomorrow.'

'Great, I'll see y—'

Click.

I look at the telephone receiver in my hand as though it has somehow just stung me.

(It has.)

The Last Drop

The Last Drop, like my fourth pint, is half empty by ten thirty and this girl – Eva – with whom I have fallen head over heels in bed and love and lust and life – having arrived late, has offered no apology, and is now sipping at an orange juice. She is tense and demure. A shadow curves sadly beneath each of her luscious green eyes. Me, I'm distantly restless; she has not yet taken her jacket off. So quickly did Eva slip into her seat by my quiet corner table I had no chance to give her the vivid hug and soft kiss that I've spent these pints mentally rehearsing.

I can feel the alcohol, raw and dark, weakening my blood, nourishing an impulse.

I've privately suspected for some time now – since before leaving Lewis – that I couldn't fall in love at all but if I could then it would be with complete devotion. I believed a couple of years ago that there was such a thing as a healthy obsession.* More bullshit has been

* Yes. Nowadays I'd only fucking believe it if it came from the mouth of a mermaid riding sidesaddle on the back of a unicorn from Mars.

written about love than about all the religions on earth. Love is an obsession, an addiction every fucking bit as powerful as alcohol, nicotine and heroin combined.

Across the pub, a barmaid winkingly wipes fresh a solitary drinker's world.

Eva seems to embody for me a perfection of modern womanhood: exotic (a native of Budapest doing her year abroad), intelligent (she's studying 'Scottish Lit, English Lit and History of Art, you know, as a Mickey Mouse subject'), beautiful (men mentally undress her as they pass in the street, women mentally knife her). She has already (unwittingly) decided for me that my busking world tour is over before it has really begun.

Now she is here and I am here and she is paying curious attention to her orange juice.

'You look just – just as beautiful as the first time I saw you,' I offer. Her eyes are underscored with sleepless dark curves, like purple wings. The eyes themselves, though, are alive with complicated patterns, they flash new and sparklingly skewed guitar solos on my heart-strings every time I look into them. 'It's great to see you,' I continue, with an extravagant smile.

Silence.

Thorny silence.

Eva pauses, doesn't look up, and begins The End by saying: 'I can't stay long. I have an essay to do for tomorrow.'

Is this a trial of my emotional resources? Like one of

those Asian temples that are built with a single deliberate flaw in order to demonstrate human imperfection in the eyes of the Creator. Of course she's allowed an imperfection; it's the proof of her near-perfection.

'Oh,' I say with pseudo-enthusiasm. 'What about?'

'Usual shite.' Her English – rather, her Scottish – is great. There's something about a multilingual woman, perhaps the unspoken acknowledgement that the world can be expressed – and seen – in more than one way, strongly implying open-mindedness, intelligence and a powerful ability to empathize.

I swallow a meditative mouthful of 80', then put the glass down on the beermat – carefully, determined to seem more sober than I am. 'Hey!' I gaze at her shining face with an earnest frown. 'What's wrong? It's been ages since we – it's been ages.'

Eva runs a gentle finger around the rim of her glass. 'Five weeks, three days.'

I wipe some 80' from my upper lip.

She draws circles around the glass.

I have some new friends. They're called Of Course I'm Fucking Jealous, Have I Fucked Up My One Chance At Actual Love, and Trembling Blue Suicide. They want to speak.

I breathe in, count onethousand twothousand three-thousand fourthousand, breathe out. 'Well – are you going to tell me what's wrong? Was it something I did? Said? *Didn't* do or say?'

215

Her hand stops. She heaves a slow, bosomy sigh. 'Look, it's really human of you to care and . . . This isn't easy.' She regards me steadily; her green eyes glitter. 'Before either of us says anything else – before I tell you what I have to tell you – I want you to know that I've gone through hell in the last few weeks, sheer *hell*.'

My heart, briefly concussed, blunders its next few beats.

'Wh-what is it? Your workload?'

Something – impatience, or anger – fizzles momentarily in her eyes.

Something else – nebulous, dreadful – tells me that my heart will never recover from the blunder, not in this life. At the same time I think it's just my imagination.

'No, not my workload.' Dragging a nervous hand through her hair, she lets out a long, calming breath. 'Look, after we – after we got together – there's no easy way to say this and *please* don't overreact, but . . . I was . . . late.'

'Late? Late for what? What are you on about? You can skive as many —'

'No. I mean *late*. With my period.'

I blanch and reach for a Pavlovian, emergency-sized swig of 80'. 'Bloody hell.' I let it sink in. '*How* late?'

'Late as in – never came.'

'Bloody fuck.' I dizzy, forced to picture a life all at sublime variance. A child. Marriage. Sleeplessness. Debt. A home. Where? '*Whe – wha – what? Are you . . . are you . . . ?*'

'*Please!* Try to stay calm. For my sake as well as your own.'

I look down at the table and recoil slightly, thinking, This is why she's on the orange juice. I lift my pint with a trembling hand. Steadying the glass, two-handedly, as a child drinks, I drain it to the last. And then burst out, 'What are we going to do? I mean, we'll have to make plans, get some money together – Jesus, I mean, what are the chances, we took precautions – we'll have to talk this through. God, I never expected this. I can't believe you're preg—'

'Slow down! Just take it easy, will you? I'm not pregnant.'

'Eh?'

I know there are some dimensions of the mysteries of womanhood with which I'll probably never be acquainted, but.

'But surely if you don't get your period that means you're pregnant?'

Her green shining eyes consider me for what seems like minutes. 'No. Just remember what I said about me going through hell, okay? I *was* pregnant . . . but I'm not now.'

A blackness dawns malevolently within me. I sink back in the seat; my head flops forward onto my chest. In an uneven murmur I say, 'And you're not talking about a miscarriage.'

'No.' Suddenly her voice modulates into a desperate

whisper, her perfect accent slipping out of gear. '*Look, I
had to have an abortion. I had no choice but to get rid of it—*'

'It?' I gasp in spiteful urgency. 'We're not talking about
throwing out a bag of rubbish. What do you think—'

'Keep your voice down, for Chrissakes. You've got
absolutely *no* idea what I've been through in the last few
weeks. We're talking about *my* body. This was inside of
me. *Me*, not you. It was *my* choice.'

I do not stop to think then, as I did later, that November
for her had been a tempestuous month: pregnancy tests,
blood tests, insomnia, a lesson in death.

'I don't believe this! You didn't even think, hey, I might
as well tell the –' I almost say 'tell the father', but the
words stall between brain and throat – 'to tell *me*. I mean,
were you even going to get in touch?'

Her breasts stare across the table, indignant, like
untouchable shields, as her eyes take on the silken blue
ripples of my shirt.

'Of course. I was just scared you might react like –
well, react like the way you *are* reacting. Or worse. I
hardly even *know* you.'

'Well *what*,' I explode, 'in the *hell* were you doing
sleeping with someone *you hardly even know*?'

Eva gives a contemptuous snort. 'Isn't that a question
you should also be asking yourself?'

I groan, rub my eyes. Of course. It is. 'Yeah, okay.
Okay, you're right. Let's talk about this sensibly. First of
all, we took precautions, so how—'

'I know we did, but obviously that didn't work. They don't have a one hundred per cent success rate. Nothing in the world's a hundred per cent.'

'No.' I shake my head. 'This is one hundred per cent fucktup.'

'*What* did you say?'

'You heard me. What do you think you're doing? This wasn't *your* choice, it was *our* choice.'

'It's *my* body. *My* life. And *my education*.' She stands bolt upright, then leans forward. '*My* fucking *choice*. If you can't deal with that then you'll just have to learn to grow up.'

'Like that poor child can't?'

I know even as I say it that it is unfair, below the belt. But I *have* said it. Eva hovers at the table, paused, as though trying to decide whether to spin on her heels and leave or say something first.

She needs the last word. '*You*,' she spits venomously, 'can stay right out of my life. Don't you *dare* get in touch with me ever *again*.'

'As if I'd *want* to stay in touch with a *murderer*.'

Almost before the last word has left my mouth, her slap has whipped across my face. At once my cheek reddens like it's been thrust into a steaming hot iron. Without a backwards glance, Eva dashes off and hurricanes out of the pub into the Grassmarket's reel and bustle.

I rub the scarlet fire in my cheek. Deep – Minch-deep

219

– within me, a tear pangs up and trembles in my right eye.

Dazed, I reach thirstily for the empty pint, my heart beating like it never has before.

The sound of the other people in the pub merges with the roar of my heart, the roar of the drinkers, a little distant, lacking the real sound and thunder of the heart's blood-tide.

It's ten past eleven and my life is over.

A Quiet Sob

I weep into my thousandpunched jacket-as-pillow, sob as quietly as I can so the other squatters won't hear. My heart feels as though it's about to burst. They say love soars then sours. Fuck. One act of love, one act of violence. I can't equate the two. I can't attribute them to the same beautiful person. I know the unborn child was a girl, and would have grown up to be as perfect as – more perfect than – Eva. For whatever has happened, Eva is still the most beautiful person I have ever met. And she has gifted me the most vital and ugly experience of my life.

A single act of love, a single act of violence?

No.

Every Month, Her Miniature Round Ghost

I write a poem for her and for me and for everyone who doesn't understand.

Every month, her miniature round ghost bleeds in your body. She was going to be my little Princess, which is why, curled sleeping in the milky white ultrasound scan of my dreamscreen, she wears a petite crown.

Golden, absurd and useless, this crown, I think, is very like hope.

She herself (vague, lucid, fragile, transparent) reminds me of a tear, a pale wee watery bubble that time's jazz and the freeflowing weather of life would transform into a pure sparkling dancing snowflake, unique and mine and fingerprint perfect.

But this snowflake, like a kiss, turned to lippy red slush. Was that deliberate on your part? For a few pads' worth of poetry, of lunar blood?

Because you forget something does not mean it didn't happen.

Do you remember spending the first nine months of your life surrounded by water?

I picture her heart beating like the smallest waves in the smallest pool that never existed.

My little mermaid, coiled like a hug of shell, seahorse-perfect; she was murdered.

She is always with me, my daughter, whose trusting gaze and unheld hand are an invisible jigsaw, whose breath is the questioning silence on the answer machine, whose mouth is the unkissed stamp on the condolence card no one knows to send.

PART THREE

A Deep and Secret Need

Letter for Kevin, with Permission to Publish

Semi-drunk in a squat,
Budapest.
Not that depressed.

Everywhere from Stornoway to Edinburgh to Paris to
Toronto to New York to Reykjavik to Moscow to Prague to
Stockholm to Amsterdam to Budapest and so on and so
forth, I experienced a phenomenon that only you, maybe,
will understand, for it isn't really sensible and it speaks of
death, perhaps magnetically.

It is this. Birds – a huge flock of birds – they fly up from
the ground, they whoosh overhead like a shower of black and
grey sparks, irresistible to my eye, whirling and cascading so
that they are no longer flying up but I am plunging down
and I can't stop looking at them even as I plummet and grow
dizzier by the instant and I know that this is what dying
must feel like and the birds seem like stunted dark angels
even as they thrust me down and they become specks in the
sky and all the innermost parts of me giddy as if readying
for a faint or even the Big Faint itself.

The experience – it's happened in every place I've ever lived – leaves me with a vertiginous intoxicated sensation that somehow – here's the part I can't explain – speaks to me of death. Kind of intriguingly.

Fuckit, I mean invitingly.

These birds, death, no longer scare me. I want to understand them, to experience what it is they imply.

My life's been a waste. Look, I want to be invisible now and as quiet as a dead man in space. Away from the gossiping eyes of Lewis, the sanctimonious judges of character who know so little of what character is outside of the ovine masses. Lewis is a place of death and if it is published my book will say something about this and also about life and about the hurt that even small 'c' conservatism brings about; conservatism is diluted fascism. I refuse to live through it. I can't live through it.

I want you, if you find a publisher, to publish the MS as we discussed. Footnotes and acknowledgements included. Write a brief introduction beginning with these words (attribute them to me): 'For some people, holding a book at arm's length simply isn't enough. If you are easily offended, consign this book to the flames immediately, or return it to the shop from which you stole it.'

(At least then we gave them fair warning.)

Ambling through Budapest's streets of doll-cute houses I've none the less had visions of tanks skulking around them like petulant wolves. Eva told me during That Night all about this city's history, a history that chimes in my mind like an awkward and necessary jazz chord, dissonant as a sneeze. Conclusion? Human history simply isn't that great an advert for our species. And as with the grand scale, so with the little fuckwit who couldn't sort his life out; there is no reason to think the future will be any different.

It's an averagely gorgeous night in Budapest. I'm staying in a (fairly) recently abandoned house – 5-star by squat standards, since it has running water. Last night a full white moon shone, very large, and I watched it for a long time as it drifted over the rooftops. I was sitting outside in the warm-ish smog at a hotel bar by the Danube, drinking malt whiskies I couldn't have afforded if I'd been planning any effort at prolonged existence. Except, of course, the moon didn't shine, it reflected borrowed light. And it wasn't large. The moon doesn't change size. It took me years to realize the illusion. The moon only appears to be big when seen in the context of being a little height above, say, a house in the distance. It's all relative. It only seems big: an optical illusion. Watch the moon rise and it gets no bigger, it merely rides above the illusion. Anyhow, a moon that seemed much bigger than normal, but wasn't, bounced its thieved sunlight onto me and I felt honoured somehow that the moon was consenting to spotlight me with so calm and realistic a beauty on my second-last night on earth and I felt so overwhelmed at the moon's graciousness and benevolence that I got up from my seat and ducked out of its light into a narrow alley, feeling embarrassed and unworthy. In the stink of the alley a thought smacked me in the brain the way

*common sense does when imagination gets in the way; the
moon was not bowed down over me: it was a scuffed dead
lightbulb that had no more sentiment or inspiration than a
creased photograph of a long-dead movie-star's face. No
longer a moon, it was a memory of other moons.*

*Tonight's sky is lit up, modestly. I remember that
conversation we had one night at the Callanish Stones, the
time we watched the sun go down and talked about the lines
you had in that poem. Remember? About how you wrote
that the dawn rose, all red and blushing embarrassed, as if it
knew it could never equal its first ever light, and so every
dawn is a failure. I've kind of felt that way inside for a long
time. My child, I think, was too pure to be born, if that
makes sense. She who was the only one who could have
made my life – luminous. (Well, her and her mother/
murderer. Yes, even now, I'm still bitter. I can't lie.) You
said some kind words at Callanish – for my benefit, I now
understand – about how the light never goes out, the sun just
travels on to light up somewhere else. Now the sky over
jaggedy Budapest is gauzy with clouds and is a blushing,
monotone red, fading where it nears the citysmog. It's fine. I
mean, it's not as though I expected fireworks or anything.
I'm happy enough with that, and I'm not going to look out
the window again.*

*Friendships have meant a lot to me. What the hell do you
think sustained me this long? But all joy – once distant – is
now gone. Everything seems indicative of a hostile universe,
like the law of diminishing returns. I wonder if death itself is a*

return? I wonder a lot about death. It's like George Willard said in Winesburg, Ohio, *'I must get myself into touch with something orderly and big that swings through the night like a star.' All or nothing? I need The Answer. Now.*

This is lucid. I'm as sane as I've ever been.

I've even drawn up all the legal documents. (Where there's a Will there's a Stornoway. Very punny, eh? The fact I can still make jokes shows how calm I am about this.)

I can tell by the way the shadows in the squat are gesturing that the sky is closing down. I'll just keep on writing until I've said it.

I've shamespiralled far enough. It's been hard on me, this weird thirst to self-destruct, and it's been harder on others. I hope that this is a selfless act, though I know it's (arguably) a selfish one. I don't know if my friends will fully understand that the days of having a drink to talk about old times or maybe to start some new ones, those days are gone – for good. One of drink's great deceptions is that good times can be orchestrated.

No one understands failure like a perfectionist – and I speak as a perfect failure.

Also, it's a little like that story you told me. Chang Tzu (spelling?) and his friend are strolling along a riverbank when Chang Tzu (yep, I've checked my notebook) says, 'Hey, look at those fish in there. They're really having fun swimming around.'

And his friend replies, 'You're not a fish. You can't know that the fish are enjoying themselves.'

Chang Tzu doesn't miss a beat. 'And you're not me. So how do you know that I don't know that the fish are enjoying themselves?'

Thus, the feeling – no, the knowledge – that my suicide is the right thing to do. You can't know it wasn't. Listen: there was nothing more you or anyone else could have done about it. Begging me to slow down my drinking was as effective as trying to shoot a whale with a water-pistol (something Eilidh might remember doing a l-o-n-g time ago). The whale was already dead.

What will I miss?

Music. (But as far as my own songs are concerned, I feel like that guy in China recently who spent fifteen years learning to fight dragons.)

Art.

Films.

Books. (Though I've read the best. The ones that are left are overwritten, overhyped or over the hill.)

Those morning swims in Edinburgh, years ago.

Eva. Very much. Still, though I know I shouldn't. I'm a romantic, in my own twisted way.

I'll miss other things too, but this life's too short now, eh, to go listing them all here.

What I won't miss is drinking my own weight in whisky. I had drink all wrong. Drink doesn't give you a better sense of who you are, it gives you a nonsense of who you are.

The bottle wasn't half full. It wasn't half empty. It was

entirely empty. Drinking alcohol is like filling yourself with emptiness.

Largely, this life has been about absence.

Absence. My life's defining presence. Loss, yes, but that implies you had something first. I don't know what I ever really had of worth.

Absence of the love I thought I needed (and Lewis told me I didn't deserve).

Absence of memory to replace some of the good times. I'm told there were more good times than I can possibly believe.

Absence of nationhood, even. Scots – genuinely – are almost twice as likely to kill themselves as their oppressor-neighbours. I'm sorry, but that figures.

Absence makes the heart grow fonder? Bullfuckingshit. When I'm alone – and I've spent most of my life alone, even in company – when I'm the only person in a ratty little squat like this the world shrinks in on me, scrutinizes me like a celestial microscope. It judges me, it judges the skanky walls around me, it judges the tension in my chest that makes my breathing so self-conscious and irregular. It judges me until there is nothing left but a judgement so solitary it seems to come from inside of me. Failure, it says. Failure. An absence, that is, of success. Absence has followed me through my life like a shadow only I can see and even then not really see but half-glimpse, glimpse enough to make me uneasier than I already was. No one ever escaped their shadow. (Except, perhaps, by becoming one.)

Absence of love. I confess a new intuition; I never really loved myself, so how could I expect to be loved? But I'm the king of the moodswingers, so I nevertheless fell immensely in love. Twice. Eva and, believe it or not, that Mystery Girl who owes me a breakfast. What did I really learn about love? Fuckit, it's like that old saying. A man with a watch always knows what time it is. A man with two watches is never sure.

Which reminds me. I've already cheated the clock, the ragged, irritating jerks of that fucking tick-tocking fucking minute hand. I've cheated it! Seriously, I'm older than I am. How?

Because alcohol actually slows down time, since the brain receives fewer pieces of information per second. Amazing! I've genuinely lived longer than I have.

(Born in one century and died in the next; there are people who lived almost to a hundred who never achieved that! And wow! This is very nearly the youngest I'll ever be!)

Then again the years mean nothing; I am still orphaned by a child who wasn't.

I had thought of starving myself to death. I think I might have enjoyed the hallucinations but the whole thing would have taken too long. I've gone a few days without food many times before, of course, but it's the thirst that really gets you. Finally, cowardice overcame wit and I decided not to starve myself in Budapest.

So much for absences – I'm replacing them with the supreme absence: absence of time.

A sickening face lolled at me today. Yeah, from inside the bathroom mirror. A couple of tears slid down my face; they looked and felt like tiny jellyfish. You know, I've considered suicide for years. Actually, I've been committing suicide for years. All I'm doing here is speeding up the process. Considerably. This way it will be less painful to others (and, maybe, myself.)

I know there are plenty people who secretly wondered how I lasted as long as I did.

I forbid mourning.

Truth is, this shouldn't be too hard because I'm already dead and as someone once said the only reason so-and-so wasn't assassinated is because there's no pleasure in killing a man who's already dead.

Not that I'm expecting it to be a whole heap of pleasure. I feel a strong guilt, which I kind of expected being a Leòdhasach and all, but it's a strange guilt because I kind of feel I'm letting some people down, which means that I've secretly believed there are people who care about me.

So I confess: I am tired of the everydayathon. I'm sick and fed up of being sickfedup (of my life: of Life). I was never one for the satisfyingness of things (other than the accoutrements of hedonism), I was never one for the melodramadness and it's all got to me. At last. That's a kind of explanation. Now, every night I take ugliness to bed (the images and memories in my head, in this book). Life has palled, become predictable for me.

I'm the kind of guy people tolerate when I'm with them, and later they tell me how much they miss me. They like me more when I'm not there. I get like that too. I like the idea of me better than me.

I've found it impossible to settle anywhere in this life. All the places I've spent any time in are so full of a sense of me that I could never live there comfortably. Anyhow, the major benefit – or cost – of being comfortable is that life seems to pass quicker. Everything's contradiction.

Understand?

Similarly, my dead child. The only way to overcome the death of a child, a child who barely got the chance to exist, is to kill yourself.

For I have a deep and secret need that she is an infant ghost in need of a ghost daddy.

Maybe like how sleep is an expansion on the darkness between blinks, so death will be a supreme extension of sleep. When I was a child, the summer days were vivid and desperate and bright. Now all that is left is an autumnal desperation and a jaded knowledge that the memory of good childhood days only exists to sharpen the contrast with the cold misery I have become as an adult. And I believe that if all my days of genuine happiness were counted and set against the days of mediocrity, unhappiness, depression and rage, then the contented days would consist of no more than a tiny percentage. I think this is true for many human beings, many more than could cope with admitting it.

I gave myself three missions to accomplish today:

Letter for Kevin, with Permission to Publish

1. Write this letter.
2. Learn a new phrase. One I'll never use in this life. But if there's an afterlife, let's say St Peter comes up to me with his celestial clipboard at the Pearly Gates, then I'll shake his angelic hand, hug him like a partygoer and boom into his cherubic lugholes *fiat experimentum in corpore vili*.
3. Exit this life via booze, blade and bath. I've already written the story . . .

Crouching down, I'll turn on the hot-water tap, feel it run cold through my fingers. I'll flick my fingers, in what will be almost a beckoning gesture, as if willing the water to warm up. Which, after a few moments, it will. I'll push the black disc of the plug into its tiny basin, swivel the tap on full and turn the cold tap on at little more than a babyish dribble.

Condensation will rise fiercely from the bathwater, mixing with the cold air, intense as coffee after ice cream.

After a few moments, the room will have warmed up considerably. I'll take my clothes off, beginning with my jacket. My skin will goosebump as I slip out of my final layers. I'll remove my watch and the silver ring Eilidh gave me on my eighteenth, remember the taps and turn them off.

This is it, then.

I lift a leg cautiously into the hot water. My foot stings like ice. I force it in to touch the bottom of the bath, moving slow as a nervous diver. The heat nips at my foot like tiny fish.

I swing and hunch down, grab the bath's side-rails, simultaneously lift my other leg off the floor and lower my body into the bathwater. It flushes my skin like an outrage.

Sinking into the heat, I whoosh a few breaths out like a boxer. My legs tingle in the burning water, my chest clutches and palpitates. Slowly I lie back, settle in. The water licks over me, a cleansing transparent smoulder.

I sink further back, let the sultry heat swim over my hair and face. It's like being in a womb, maybe – surrounded by water, powerless, a liquid sleep before the great, insurgent sea-change.

My thinking is so calm – taking a bath seems such a humdrum piece of domesticity – that for a fraction of a second I almost change my mind.

For a moment I feel watery and weak and useless, like non-alcoholic beer.

But, no.

Why should a person be loved when he hasn't loved himself? And how could I love myself when I don't even know myself? This is serious.

Sacrifice. My final act is courageous and unselfpitying. I can be proud of myself at least once.

The words, the words through which I've attempted to engage with my self-esteem, were so many windchimes in a tornado.

Joyce – was it? 'Love loves to love love.' Sounds great. What does it mean? I had tried so hard to—

Never mind. No digression. It's time to do it.

I sit bolt upright with a gasp of determination. My face feels blue. Water drips from my hair, streams down my face, runs silently over my body. I scrunch my eyes and rub them.

Steel yourself.

It's time.

I take a few deep breaths to calm my sprinting heart. I reach over and pick up the knife. Every moment is slowed down, everything is shiningly vivid. And yet, my hand is not shaking. I am not anxious. I am in control of myself.

There is a certain excitement buzzing like adrenalin all over my body.

I hold the knife in my right hand, then realize – duh – it would make more sense to use the left hand first.

A blip of panic.

The knife quivers in my weaker hand. I fix the knife with a tight-eyed stare, regulate my breathing again. Focus, man, focus.

In the bathroom's quiet, the only sounds are my heart's kettledrum beats and the occasional drip-drup of water droplets diving home, sending little ripples of excitement like gossip around them.

Remember: this is bravery.

Everybody thinks about this, but very few have the ability to do it.

Do it.

I clench my fist around the knife and bring the blade to my wrist. It's cold on my skin. I push down slightly on the knife and – with a fat, hot snake's bite – the blade dives into

my skin. For a moment, as blood spills around the incision, I
feel wronged, as though someone else has, unbelievably,
stuck a knife in me. But it's important to be quick. I push
the knife in further, then pull it in an agony along my skin –
three inches, but feels much, much longer. The knife does not
travel as easily as I had expected, entangled by depth and
resilience.

For a second a darkness flashes in my eyes. My wrist feels
as though it has been forced into a furnace. I want to
withdraw the knife, but I've decided. Withdrawal
is not what I want; or, it is a withdrawal from the
unhappiness of life, a withdrawal that can only be bought
with pain. The blood flows from my wrist in a swift little
waterfall. Wow, the bathwater is already turning red. I swap
the knife over to my right hand, but find that my grip on it is
clumsy and weak as a child's.

My breathing is difficult, panicked, inefficient. I am
determined not to scream, not to cry. Why do people cry in
pain? In order to attract attention – to demand solace and
sympathy from a loved one. The pain in my wrist has spread
up my arm to my brain and my heart, like a quick poison,
evil and uncompromising.

With a great effort I jab the knife into my left wrist,
awkwardly. It does not sink in deeply, and seems sorer this
time, maybe because I'm expecting the pain. I try to push it
along my wrist but I'm so weak – not just my right arm, my
right side – I'm so dizzy and weak all over now that I can't
force the knife to go very far. I've surely done enough. Tiny

white stars are sparkling around me like strobed snowflakes.
It looks magical, a little lightshow to divert me from the
pain. I look at the knife eating into my left wrist. I pull it
out, amazed that real things can still be seen and felt as
though they are everyday objects and not witnesses to
something stupendous.

I drop the knife over the side of the bath, crinng, onto the
floor.

The last candle is glowing and breathing steadily. I like
its peace.

Now snowflakes dance all around it, minuscule doves.

A pain is rumbling through my head, a deep bass pain to
counterpoint – is that the word? – the highpitched screaming
in my wrists.

My life is flowing out of me.

There is a great dark tide inside me, buffeting.

I lower my arms into the water, feel the pain flare then
subside to a fierce kissing in the liquid heat.

A smile spreads across my face. I probably look like an
imbecile. My thoughts are slow, becoming slower. I didn't
scream. I didn't cry.

I did something right in my life.

I have

almost dimmed

into the great whatever.

A hot and darkening mist is gathering about me, like
people crowding a cot.

*

Fuck, it's nearly morning. Already the sun is rising and plainly – I don't need to look out the window – it's beautiful, more beautiful than the most beautiful simile you could et cetera.

She is an infant ghost in need of a ghost daddy.

I am glad I have accomplished these writings.

Now I can kill myself without blushing.

Roman Stornoway

Romance torn away

We are who we are because we grew up the Stornoway way. We do not live in the back of beyond we live in the very heart of beyond.

Acknowledgements

One

Very few animals were harmed during the production of this book (an enormous whale that was already dead, a bunch of fish for nutritional purposes), though quite a few trees were sent to an afterlife they had surely never conceived of.

My clothing and that of most of the main characters was provided by local charity shops. Accessories – including but not limited to – rings, T-shirts, bracelets, necklaces and hats – were DIY and many of them pretty cool too, I can tell you. (If you wear 'label' clothing then you're a moron. Didn't your parents ever teach you how to dress *yourself*?)

Tattoos were done by registered professionals and the same is more or less true of piercings.

I'd like to thank everyone who knows me. But I can't.

I'd like to apologize to most people who know me. But I can't.

I'd like to decide what kind of albums people buy. But I can't. *Sin agad e. C'est la* fucking *vie*.

Now the main man. This book wouldn't exist without the patience of Kevin MacNeil. Kevin, I owe you bigtime, and not just for the literary/practical/hellevenpsychiatric help. You brought me focus and peace when I didn't even realize I fucking needed them. (Psychiatry's polite; desperation isn't.) That said, I know you'll forgive me for saying that I'm glad everyone in the world doesn't have the same sense of humour as you. Weird fucking jokes, man.

It was also a pleasure taking some classes from someone who's a black belt in haiku.

If I see you in some afterlife which I don't believe in then I'll eat one of your fucking hats, *a charaid. Thoir an aire ort fhèin. Tsheeuree.*

R. Stornoway

2004

Two

I want principally to thank the man known herein as R. Stornoway for his honesty from the beginning; in retrospect, creating this book was as much a learning process for me as it was for him. The distinction between lessons in literature and lessons in life often blurred during our meetings, phone calls and emails, and that's probably how it should be – especially if one submits, as I do, to Wallace Stevens' philosophy: 'Literature is the better part of life. To this it seems inevitably necessary to add, provided life is the better part of literature.'

I'd like to thank Judy Moir for all her help throughout my publishing career and for being the finest editor in the country.

Thanks to the Scottish Arts Council for the Writer's Bursary.

Special thanks to everyone (family, old friends, new acquaintances) in my home town of Stornoway, Scotland, for allowing me time and space to work on R. S.'s manuscript, a job that was unexpectedly fulfilling and . . . well, *different* from my usual writing duties. If my work on this book further decelerated completion of my novel *Singing for the Blue Men*, then I can at least say that *The Stornoway Way*'s demands were welcome distractions rather than frustrating intrusions. Two quite different literary intensities will sometimes work to alleviate each other's pressures, and that was certainly the case here. My joy at discovering a new literary voice from my native island was inestimable. There are few – too few – writers of any generation currently representing the Outer Hebrides. I sincerely hope R. S. is the first of many diverse new Hebridean voices, Gaelic and English, old and young, classical and wild, to square up to the world.

Kevin MacNeil

2005

K. M. *www.KevinMacNeil.com*

R. S. RIP